Copyright © 2025 Lisa
The Healthiest Corpse in the Morgue and Other Short Stories.

All rights reserved. No part of this book may be reproduced, stored in any form, or transmitted by any means—whether by shadow, whisper, or machine—without prior written permission of the authors, except for brief passages quoted in reviews.

This is a work of fiction. Though its ghosts may feel familiar, all names, characters, places, and incidents arise from the authors' imagination. Any resemblance to actual persons, living or dead, is purely coincidental... and entirely unintended.

Editor: Lisa Bentley
Cover Design: Lisa Bentley
Internal Layout: Lisa Bentley

ISBN:
First Edition

For permissions, contact: arabellaparke@yahoo.com

Printed in the United Kingdom, where old stories linger and the past is never fully silent.

Authors photograph by Joanne Elizabeth Portraits.

This is a work of fiction. Names, characters, locations, events, and incidents are either the product of the author's imagination or are used fictitiously. Any resemblance to actual persons, living or deceased, or to real events, places, or organisations is purely coincidental and unintended.

The stories contained within explore themes of the supernatural, psychological unease, and imagined realities. They are intended solely for entertainment and literary purposes. No part of this book should be interpreted as factual, instructional, or advisory.

The author and publisher assume no responsibility for any interpretations, beliefs, or actions taken by readers as a result of engaging with this work.

Also by Arabella Parke

Daughters of Ash and Sorrow and Other Supernatural Thrillers.

For Phyllis and Peter Jackson

& Maureen and Terry Bentley

Content

- Copyright
- Introduction
- The Healthiest Corpse in the Morgue
- The Dolls House Players
- The Man Who Knew Everything
- About the Author
- Coming Soon

Like many, I believe nobody ever truly leaves us. When we say goodbye for the final time, I believe there is a whisper against our ear, a soft reassurance that we are not really parting. We go peacefully, content in the knowledge that we will still linger close to those we love — our family, our friends, and yes, even our beloved pets and the creatures with whom we've shared our hearts.

While we wait for our loved ones to join us — or while we bask in the company we have longed for — we find ways to send little hints, gentle signs, quiet reminders that our presence endures, and our love still flows.

The stories I create are tales that explore those signs.

What follows is a collection of stories that linger in the spaces between worlds, where love leaves fingerprints, memory refuses to fade, and not every whisper is meant to comfort. .

Some are unsettling.

And some… well, some might be voices we'd rather not hear from again.

arabella x

… The Healthiest Corpse in the Morgue

Chapter 1

The hall smelled of polish, instant coffee, and those pink wafer biscuits that appear at every church event whether they're wanted or not. Somewhere a kettle clicked, echoing against the high ceiling, and the last few chairs scraped into place.

Rows of metal seats faced a makeshift stage about two feet high, draped in a slightly crooked purple cloth that shimmered in the strip-lighting. Paper bunting from last month's jumble sale still hung across the beams, spelling out **WELCOME** in fading felt-tip.

At the centre stood Peggy Morpeth, blonde hair set to perfection, blouse a riot of carnations. She held the microphone like a born entertainer and smiled at her audience — sixty-odd locals, fanning themselves with programmes and expectation.

"Well," she said, eyes twinkling, "the spirit worlds got a better turnout than the parish council meeting. Let's hope they're better behaved."

A ripple of laughter broke the tension; the nervous energy softened into something expectant. Peggy always opened with humour — it made people comfortable before the tears began. She closed her eyes, swaying slightly, one hand drifting as if testing a current in the air.

"I'm feeling a presence," she murmured. "A man, mid-fifties, smells faintly of engine oil. That mean anything to anyone?"

A hand shot up in the third row. "My Alan! He was a mechanic!"

Peggy smiled kindly. "Ah yes, he says he's proud of how you kept his tools clean, even if you never could work out what half of them did."

The woman burst into tears; the crowd sighed. Someone passed her a tissue, and a few others sniffed in sympathy.

Peggy moved smoothly from one spirit to the next — a grandmother who'd hidden sweets in the airing cupboard, a lad who'd crashed his motorbike but still watched *Match of the Day* "from the cheap seats."

Each message was gentle, funny, comforting. The audience gasped, wept, whispered. Peggy's voice floated like perfume — soft, reassuring, just mystical enough to make believers of them all.

She paused once, letting the silence bloom before speaking again, the way a singer leaves a note hanging in the rafters. "They're not gone, loves," she said softly. "They've just stepped into another room."

By the end of the evening, people were hugging strangers. A woman in a floral dress said, "You've a gift, love. Truly touched by the angels." Peggy dabbed her brow with a tissue. "Oh, they do all the work, my dear. I'm just the telephone line."

As the crowd drifted out into the warm Essex night, some still dabbing their eyes, others laughing in that giddy, post-séance way, Peggy gathered her things.

Two ladies from the Women's Guild insisted on hugging her goodbye, leaving smudges of lipstick on her cheeks.

"Life is eternal, my love," she said gently to one. "They never really leave us."

When the last door closed, the hall seemed to exhale — folding chairs gleaming, air still tinged with perfume and floor polish. Peggy looked back once, half expecting a whisper from the empty stage, then smiled at her own foolishness and turned off the lights.

Home Comforts

The bungalow kitchen was bright with floral curtains and the smell of something Kevin had burnt. The clock ticked cheerfully above the sink; the cat, Ruby, curled near the Aga, unimpressed.

Kevin sat at the table with a ledger and a mug of tea.

"How'd it go then, Mystic Peg?" he said, grinning over the rim.

Peggy slipped off her shoes. "Lovely crowd. Emotional, mind you. Half of 'em needed tissues; other half needed gin."

Kevin chuckled. "That's eight months you're booked solid now. You'll be charging the spirits overtime soon."

She kissed his head fondly. "They don't charge, love. Just whisper."

He leaned back, pleased with himself. "And we listen — for a small fee, mind."

Peggy rolled her eyes but smiled. He'd helped her with the website, the flyers, the bookings. He liked the bustle and the money, but mostly he liked seeing her light up under those stage lights.

Later, when he'd gone to bed, Peggy sat alone for a while, flipping through her diary — Thursday, the restaurant gig. Fancy crowd, she'd been told. Three courses and prosecco. She'd need to polish her stories a bit for that one.

Outside, the wind rattled the gate. The clock ticked on. For a moment she thought she heard a soft hum, like a radio tuning itself, but it was only the kettle cooling on the counter.

Dinner with the Departed

The restaurant gleamed — white linen pristine as snow, chandeliers dripping gold like frozen honey, the faint clink of glasses and the hush of polite laughter knitting the air into something warm and velvety. Waiters glided like swans, plates balanced effortlessly, silk-footed and silent, as though the entire dining room were performing a ballet.

Peggy stood just off-centre, by a tiny, raised stage near the dessert trolley. A strawberry gateau wobbled by as she adjusted her mic, clutching it not with fear but a performer's intimate familiarity, as though it were the hand of an old friend. Her blouse sparkled under the lights — sequins catching even the shallow breaths. Her nerves, though, did not sparkle. They fizzed, crackled, threatened to spill out of her pores. But she swallowed them like a professional.

"I've a lady with me," she began, eyes half-closed as though she were listening to the sea inside her skull. Her voice was gentle, steady, the voice of someone who has soothed children and frightened adults. "Catherine... or maybe Margaret? A kind soul, hospital bed, chest trouble, couldn't quite catch her breath at the end."

A woman at table seven jerked upright, napkin falling into her soup. A gasp escaped her. "Oh my God, that's Aunt Meg! She died of emphysema!"

Peggy opened her eyes, soft and knowing. "She's with you, my love. Still fussing that you don't wear a scarf. She says she can't help herself."

A beat of stunned silence — and then the woman laughed, though tears gathered like tiny beads of salt. Others around her smiled, touched by something gentle, something old and aching. Peggy rode the moment perfectly — one part sympathy, one part stagecraft, spinning sentiment into performance like a seamstress threading silk.

"She's showing me yellow curtains," Peggy continued, holding her breath as though clarifying the vision. "And a little dog with a ridiculous haircut. She says he still waits by the door."

The table erupted, half laughter, half sobs. Even strangers felt the tug. Grief became communal, transformed, tamed for a moment. Peggy let them have it — the humour, the tenderness, the ache — and they drank it like warm wine.

When the set was over, the room didn't collapse back into ordinary chatter. Instead, it leaned toward her — chairs scraping, bodies turning, hearts softening. A queue formed, serpentine and reverent. People clasped her hands, both of hers, as though they might absorb some of her gift. Cheeks damp, breath hitching, they whispered words into her ear: amazing, blessing, real connection. Their voices trembled, but there was relief in them, too — like someone had peeled back a bandage and let healing air inside.

Peggy smiled, her voice all warmth and tea-cosy wisdom, like a favourite aunt handing out biscuits. "They never truly go," she told them. "They just whisper when you're quiet enough to listen."

Outside, the night pressed close against the restaurant windows — black, gleaming, expectant, as though the darkness itself wanted to lean in and hear more. Peggy did not see the faint flicker in the mirrored bar behind her, didn't notice the subtle shift of a shadow that should not have been moving. Nor did she see the wineglass that trembled ever so slightly on its slender stem, quivering like someone had just walked past — someone only she would have recognised.

Chapter 2

The Private Sitting

The Morpeths' front room looked like a cross between a tearoom and a gift shop. Doilies on every surface, two china angels on the mantelpiece, and the faint scent of lavender polish mingling with plug-in air freshener.

At the centre stood a small round table draped with purple velvet, a single candle flickering in a glass holder, and a bowl of crystals that Peggy swore were "charged under the full moon," though in truth they came from the garden centre's home décor aisle.

She fluffed a cushion, adjusted the light, and pressed *play* on her CD player. Gentle ocean waves rolled through the room, punctuated by the occasional distant seagull.

The doorbell rang.

"Come in, my love!" Peggy called.

Mrs. Whitlow appeared — a round, anxious woman in her sixties clutching a handbag shaped like a cat. Her eyes were already red-rimmed.

"Oh, Mrs. Morpeth, thank you for seeing me at such short notice," she said, voice trembling. "It's about my Ken. I just can't seem to settle."

Peggy's smile was warm enough to melt butter. "Of course, dear heart. Sit yourself down. I'll pop the kettle on — spirits work better when everyone's comfortable."

A few minutes later, with tea poured and tissues ready, Peggy closed her eyes and took a deep, theatrical breath.

"Right," she murmured. "Let's see who's come through tonight."

She tilted her head, frowning slightly, the way television mediums do when listening to invisible company.

"I'm feeling a presence," she said softly. "Strong man, kind eyes, smells faintly of... tomato feed. Gardening, yes? Always tinkering with something. He says— oh! — he's still cross about the shed door."

Mrs. Whitlow gasped, a hand flying to her mouth. "That's my Ken! He hit his thumb on that door the week before he… oh, bless him!"

Peggy nodded gently, eyes closed, expression serene. "He's smiling now, love. Says you've done wonders with the runner beans, though you're over-watering the geraniums again. He's showing me a cardigan — green, maybe brown — very loved."

Tears rolled freely now. "He wore that every day!"

"Of course he did. Still does." Peggy's voice dropped to a hush. "He says he doesn't want you to be sad. Says the garden's not the same without your singing."

Mrs. Whitlow laughed and sobbed at once. "I do sing to the plants! Oh, Ken…"

The session went on for half an hour, a gentle dance of grief and comfort. Peggy's tone shifted from reverent to light, offering small jokes, tiny reassurances, and the soft rhythm of closure.

When it was over, Mrs. Whitlow squeezed her hand. "You've no idea what this means to me."

Peggy smiled sweetly. "It's all right, my love. They never really leave us. Just… change address."

When the front door closed and the ocean-sound CD wound down to silence, Peggy exhaled. She leaned back in her chair and kicked off her slippers, face calm but eyes alert.

On the little table beside her lay an open notebook — neat columns of tidy handwriting:

Kenneth Whitlow – allotment society – accident with shed door – cardigan, greenish – heart failure, age 72.

She flipped to another page, filled with names, dates, and phrases: *loved the sea, hospital bed, church choir, missing wedding ring.*

The notes were taken from obituaries in the *Essex Gazette*, Facebook memorial pages, and whispers overheard at the supermarket.

She tapped her pen against the paper, humming. Preparation, she always said, was respect for Spirit. And if it also made the readings smoother — well, everyone benefited, didn't they?

Kevin appeared in the doorway, yawning, pint glass in hand.

"All right, Mystic Peg? Another satisfied customer?"

"Very," she said, smiling faintly. "Ken popped in to say hello."

Kevin chuckled, dropping onto the sofa. "He can pop in anytime if he keeps paying like that. That's sixty quid, love — you're wasted on the church halls. We ought to get you on telly."

"Don't be daft," Peggy said, but her eyes gleamed. "I'm not after fame."

"No, just fortune." He winked. "You keep this up; I'll have that new caravan before summer."

She swatted him with a tea towel, laughing, but when he'd gone to bed, her face grew thoughtful.

———

That night, long after Kevin had gone to bed, Peggy sat under the yellow pool of her lamp. Her notebook lay open:

AGE – ILLNESS – CAUSE – DETAILS.

Beside it, library books stacked high:
Common Respiratory Conditions, End-of-Life Care, Understanding Dementia, Accidents and Trauma.

She adjusted her glasses, turned a page, and began to read.

Outside, the wind brushed against the windowpane with a slow, sighing sound — like someone whispering her name.

Chapter 3

The Comforters

The hospitals were Peggy's favourite kind of quiet. That soft hum of machines, the scent of disinfectant and flowers; the way everyone spoke in whispers as though the walls themselves might bruise.

She walked those corridors like she belonged there — pastel scarf, kind eyes, a notebook tucked under one arm. Kevin trailed behind carrying her handbag and a box of supermarket biscuits.

They started with the hospice at Colchester. Peggy signed the visitor book with a flourish, adding *Spiritual Worker* under "Reason for Visit." The volunteer on reception smiled. "Oh, how lovely. You do such wonderful work."

Peggy touched her heart modestly. "We just bring comfort, dear. That's all anyone wants, isn't it?"

Kevin coughed into his hand. "And a cuppa if there's one going."

The pair moved softly from room to room — gentle smiles, light touches on shoulders. Peggy leaned close to each bedside, her voice low and melodic.

"Don't you worry, love. The angels are close. They'll see you safe when it's time."

Family members wept, grateful for any kindness. Before she left, Peggy always pressed a small cream card into someone's hand.

PEGGY MORPETH – Spiritual Medium. Messages of Hope and Healing.

"If ever I can help," she'd whisper. "Afterwards, I mean."

Kevin waited by the lifts, jingling coins in his pocket. "How many cards you got left, Peg?"

"Half a dozen. We'll need more printed. And don't hover, you look like a debt collector."

They visited every Thursday. One week it was the hospice; the next, the geriatric ward. Peggy brought biscuits for the nurses, said she was offering "pastoral support." The staff adored her — her cheer, her gossip, her way of remembering names.

But she remembered other things, too.

The conditions written on the whiteboard at the end of each bed, the family photographs pinned to noticeboards, the names and dates on the Get-Well cards. Each detail found its way into her notebook later that night. Age, illness, family connections, hobbies, nicknames. All lovingly catalogued under *Future Contacts*.

Sometimes, Kevin waited in the hospital café, flicking through racing tips on his phone.

"She's got a heart of gold, my wife," he told anyone who'd listen. "Helps people through the hardest bit, she does. Not everyone can talk to the other side, you know."

When Peggy reappeared, cheeks flushed and voice husky from all the soft consolations, he held her coat for her like a stage manager between acts.

"Good morning's work?" he'd say.

Peggy would smile, slipping the visitor badge into her pocket.

"Let's just say," she'd murmur, "the lines are staying open."

Chapter 4

Helping Hands

The caravan brochure was spread out across the kitchen table like a treasure map. Kevin jabbed a finger at the page. "Look at that — new awning, built-in shower, proper mattress. None of your inflatable rubbish."

Peggy poured the tea. "We've already got a caravan."

He snorted. "We've got a tin box that leaks when it rains and smells of gas when it doesn't. This—" he tapped the glossy page "—this is freedom."

"Freedom costs twenty-two grand," she said.

He sighed, flipping through his ledger. "Bookings are slowing, Peg. Everyone's on that TikTik nonsense now — online mediums, bloody filters and fairy lights. Half the town's talking to their dead nan through a ring light."

Peggy smiled, but it was tight. "We'll pick up. Word of mouth always does."

Kevin leaned back, chair creaking. "Maybe we can help it along a bit, eh? Give fate a nudge."

She looked at him over her glasses. "What's that supposed to mean?"

He shrugged, grinning. "We've been visiting that hospice regular, haven't we? Being comforting. If one or two of 'em… you know… move along, it's not like we're killing anyone. Just… tidying the waiting room."

"Kevin!"

"Don't 'Kevin' me, Peg. You said yourself they're half in the next world already."

She hesitated — long enough for him to see the thought take root.

Two nights later, the hospital car park glistened under sodium lights. Peggy's floral coat swished nervously as she hurried across the tarmac. Kevin carried a clipboard and a fake ID badge he'd printed at home. It read: **Maintenance Assistant – K. Morpeth.**

"Keep your head down," he whispered.

"I feel ridiculous."

"You look professional."

They slipped inside through a side door left ajar for smokers. The corridor smelt of disinfectant and loneliness.

"Third on the left," Kevin murmured. "Old boy with the emphysema. We've seen him twice."

Peggy's heels clicked on the lino, each step louder than it should have been. She paused at the bedside, heart pounding. The patient slept fitfully, lips grey, chest rattling like a loose hinge.

Peggy leaned close. "You've suffered enough, love," she whispered, brushing a hand over his forehead. "The angels are waiting."

Kevin fiddled with the tubing. One swift twist — a hiss, a silence. The machine's steady beep stumbled, then stopped.

Peggy shut her eyes. "Go in peace."

They stood for a moment, the only sound the distant shuffle of nurses. Then Kevin tugged her sleeve. "Come on, Florence Night-murder. Let's scarper."

Back home, the kettle whistled, absurdly cheerful. Kevin slumped in his chair, grinning. "Well, that's one for the spirit world. Should drum up business once he starts chatting."

Peggy didn't answer. Her hands trembled as she stirred her tea. She could still feel the warmth leaving the old man's skin — the exact second when the room seemed to sigh.

That night, she dreamt of whispering voices.

Not her usual gentle chorus, but a low murmur, too many to count, just beyond hearing. When she woke, the house was silent except for the faint hum of the fridge — and, she thought, something else.

A breath.

Just behind her ear.

Chapter 5

Whispers in the Line

Business increased, and by the end of the month, Peggy Morpeth was Basildon's most in-demand medium. Posters went up in shop windows

— *An Evening with Peggy: Messages from Beyond (Tea & Biscuits Included).*

Her phone rang off the hook. Kevin handled the bookings, his grin widening with every call.

"Full house again next Thursday," he said, waving the diary. "You'll have to start turning 'em away."

Peggy smiled, though her hands ached from holding the microphone too long. "Bless 'em. People do need hope."

"And we need that caravan," Kevin said. "Spirit world's paying for the upgrade."

He was joking. Mostly.

That night's event was in a golf club function room, all mirrored walls and faint smell of Febreze. Peggy worked the crowd like a pro. "I'm getting a George — very stubborn, liked his garden just so."

A woman gasped. "That's my husband!"

Peggy smiled warmly. "He's telling me you've been watering the roses too much. Says they're drowning."

Laughter through tears — always the sweet spot.

But as she spoke, something shifted.

A low hum in her ear, almost electrical.

Then, beneath her own words, another voice — quiet but unmistakable.

"Liar."

Peggy faltered, covering with a cough. "Ooh, bit of a tickle tonight. Spirits must've caught me cold."

The audience laughed, unaware.

She pressed on, the warmth in her voice wobbling only slightly. But the whisper stayed — faint, insistent, threading through every sentence.

"You took me."

By the end, her hands were shaking so badly she could barely sign autographs.

At home, Kevin counted the cash. "Three hundred and forty! Not bad for an hour's chat with the afterlife."

Peggy poured herself a brandy. "Did you… hear anything? While I was talking?"

He looked up. "Like what?"

"Nothing," she said quickly. "Just tired."

She went to bed early, but sleep refused her. The whisper came again, closer now — as if the air itself leaned in.

A chorus, not one voice.

Soft. Angry.

"You sent me too soon."

She sat up, heart pounding. The shadows of the room seemed to breathe. From the kitchen, she heard a creak. Footsteps — slow, deliberate — crossing the floor.

Then the kettle clicked on.

Peggy clutched the duvet. Kevin snored beside her, dead to the world.

A moment later, the smell of burning toast drifted across the room.

Chapter 6

The Night Rounds

Peggy had tried to ignore the voices. She'd lit candles, said prayers, even told Kevin she was taking a "spiritual detox." But every night, as soon as the lights went out, the whispers came back — soft, wet sounds in the dark.

"You took him."

"You took me too soon."

She'd sit bolt upright, clutching the duvet. "Oh, shut up," she hissed into the dark. "You're not even *real*."

But the air would shift, heavy as breath. Somewhere, deep in the plumbing, water dripped in slow, accusing beats.

Kevin was the first to break the silence over breakfast.

"Bookings are tailing off," he said, buttering his toast like it had offended him. "You've done half the county, Peg. People move on."
He looked up. "Maybe it's time to give the spirits a nudge, eh?"

Peggy stared. "You mean—?"

He gave a half-smile. "Well. There's no harm in reminding the world that people are dying all the time."

That evening, they drove to St. Agnnes Hospital, headlights cutting through the mist.

Peggy wore a nurse's cardigan and a worried expression. Kevin had a clipboard and the confidence of a man who never second-guessed himself.

The corridors were mostly empty. A night nurse nodded to them as they passed.

"Visiting late?"

"End-of-life comfort work," Peggy said smoothly, flashing her laminated card. "Spiritual Volunteer Service."

The nurse smiled wearily and kept walking.

They stopped outside a ward they'd been to the week before — Room 12, the old sailor with the oxygen mask, and Room 14, the woman who'd clutched Peggy's hands and begged her to "keep the light on in the other side."

Peggy hesitated. "Kev… maybe this is—"

"Quick in, quick out," he said. "Peaceful, like you said."

He pulled the curtain around the bed. Machines blinked quietly in the dim light. Peggy's reflection wavered in the monitor screen, pale and trembling.

Kevin's hand hovered over the switch. "On three," he said. "You do the talking bit."

She swallowed. "You're going home to the angels now love," she whispered. "Begin your journey in peace…"

A long tone filled the room. The screen went flat green.

They stood there for a moment, neither speaking. Then Kevin exhaled. "Well," he said, "business should pick up."

Peggy stared at the body. For a second, she thought she saw the chest rise again — not with air, but with something darker. A ripple, like a breath from deep water.

She stumbled back. "Did you see—?"

But Kevin was already halfway to the door. "Come on, Peg. We've got another one."

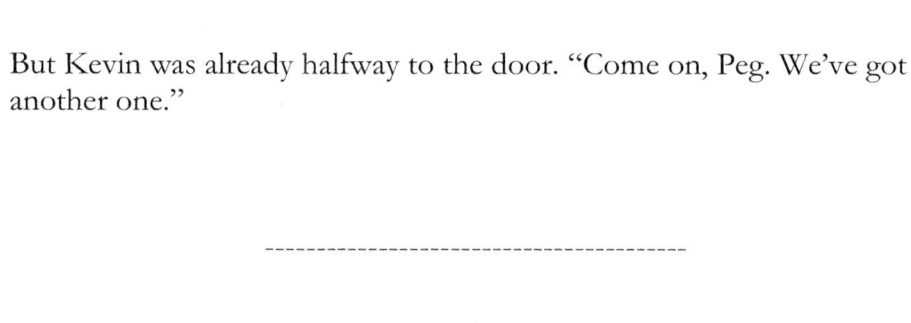

By the time they reached the car park, the rain had started. Peggy's hands shook so badly she dropped the keys twice.

As Kevin lit a cigarette, she looked up at the hospital windows — dark squares against the wet sky. In one of them, she swore she saw a figure standing. Thin, grey, watching.

When she blinked, it was gone.

Chapter 7

The Ones You Took

The hall smelled of polish and stale tea — same as ever. Rows of folding chairs faced the stage, the purple cloth still slightly crooked from last time. The urn in the corner hissed like an impatient ghost. Someone coughed, another shuffled a chair. The place had its own kind of breathing.

Peggy Morpeth stood centre stage, sequins catching the strip-light glare, microphone poised, smile fixed.

"Well," she said brightly, "lovely to see so many familiar faces! The spirit world's queueing up tonight, my loves. We'd better not keep them waiting. They don't like to be kept waiting, trust me — they'll start moving the chairs again."

A ripple of polite laughter rolled through the hall, though it sounded thinner than usual. Peggy's eyes swept the crowd — there was Mrs Ellis, front row as always, dabbing her eyes already; the florist twins, clutching their handbags like shields. But something was off. The air felt heavy, the sort that pressed on your shoulders.

She took a steadying breath. "Let's see who's here with us."

She found her rhythm quickly. A man's watch left by the sink, a mother's perfume, a lost dog who still slept on the landing. The crowd leaned in, warm and murmuring — the usual magic taking hold.

"There's a young lad here — says he's still cheering for West Ham, bless him. Anyone?"

Laughter, a few hands raised. Peggy smiled. Easy. Familiar. Safe.

"All right, now I've another — a gentleman, mid-forties, maybe fifties. Heart trouble, sudden passing. Does that sound right to anyone?"

Silence. Then a hesitant voice: "My brother—"

Peggy nodded, relieved. "Yes, that's him, love. He says he's—"

Her words stopped. The microphone gave a low hum, like a groan through the speakers.

"He says he's what?" someone called.

Peggy blinked. Her throat tightened. She could hear another sound now, faint but clear, close to her ear.

"You took him!"

She froze.

The crowd murmured. Kevin, standing near the back, frowned. Peggy forced a laugh. "Spirits do love their drama," she said, shaking her head. "Always think they're on the telly."

A few people chuckled nervously. Peggy closed her eyes again, grasping for the easy rhythm of her patter.

"All right, I've another presence here — a kind lady, hospital bed, she says she—"

"You took me too soon!"

The microphone cracked sharply. A few people jumped. Peggy's voice wavered.

"She—she's just saying she's at peace—"

"It wasn't my time!"

The lights flickered. The air seemed to pulse, cold then hot. Someone whispered, "Is this part of it?"

Another, louder: "She don't look right!"

Peggy's hands trembled around the mic. She tried to smile, but her reflection wavered in the chrome of the stand — and behind her own eyes, she saw others.

Faces pale and hollow. Hospital faces.

Breathing masks. Plastic tubes, then she heard the faint beep of machines.

"You took us."

She stumbled back, hitting the stool behind her. The mic screeched — a shrill wail that made people clap their hands to their ears. A woman fainted. Someone shouted, "Get the lights!"

Kevin was already pushing through the rows. "Peg, end it! End it now!"

But Peggy didn't move. Her gaze was fixed on the far end of the hall, near the fire exit. In the dark beyond the doorway, a handful of shapes stood motionless. Still as shadows — yet their eyes shone like glass in water.

And she knew them.

The ward. The machines. The smell of bleach and lilies.

A voice drifted from somewhere close — quiet, almost tender: "Peg… Peg, why did you touch that switch?"

Her heart thudded. "Kevin," she whispered, "they're here. The ones from the hospital."

Then the lights snapped back to full. The hall looked ordinary again — rows of chairs, people muttering, frightened, gathering their coats. Half the audience had gone. The rest avoided her eyes.

Kevin reached her, grabbed her arm. "Come on. Let's go."

Outside, the night air was damp and cold.

"They were there," she said, her voice small. "Kevin, they were there."

He swallowed. "You're just tired, Peg. That's all. You need a rest."

She nodded, though she didn't believe it.

That night, long after Kevin had gone to bed, Peggy sat before her dressing table. The lamp gave a weak, yellow glow. Her reflection floated dimly in the mirror — pale, uncertain.

The clock ticked. Somewhere, a floorboard sighed. She rubbed her temples, eyes heavy. Then she heard it — soft, close, almost gentle: the sound of breathing that wasn't hers.

Her reflection leaned closer, though she hadn't moved.

And just by her ear, a whisper — thin as air, cold as metal:

"You took me too soon."

The lamp flickered. The breath stopped.
Peggy sat perfectly still, staring into the dark glass —

— until her reflection blinked. And she didn't.

Chapter 8

Night Shift

The bungalow was too quiet. Not peaceful — the wrong kind of quiet, like the air was listening. The fridge hummed, the clock ticked, and Peggy Morpeth sat bolt upright in bed, staring into the dark.

Beside her, Kevin snored — that rasping, uneven sort of snore that always made her want to throw a pillow at his head. She tried to shut her eyes, but every time she did, she saw faces.

Pale faces. Hospital faces.

You took me too soon.

She sat up again, sweating. "Stop it," she muttered into the dark. "Just stop it."

From under the duvet came Kevin's muffled voice.

"If you're talking to me, Peg, it's too bloody late. I'm asleep."

She sighed. "Can't rest. Not after last night."

"Then don't think about it," he said, half-asleep. "Wasn't real anyway. They were just—"

"They were there, Kev. In the hall. I saw 'em."

He groaned, turning over. "You and your nerves. You're wound tighter than me mother's curlers. You'll be believing you can actually speak to spirits next!"

That stung. Peggy turned away, folding her arms. The dark seemed to thicken around her. There was a pause. Then Kevin's tone shifted — lighter, coaxing.

"Look, love. You were brilliant. The crowd'll be back next week, don't you worry. But if we want that caravan by spring, we need to get the bookings up again."

She frowned. "You think I don't know that?"

"Then let's do another round at the hospital," he said softly. "For comfort. Just a few visits. Remind folk what you do. Bit of goodwill — and maybe a few new clients."

Peggy hesitated. The whisper from the séance still echoed in her ears. But Kevin was smiling that charming, crooked smile of his — the one that had got her into half her bad decisions.

"Oh, all right," she said finally. "Just a few."

They dressed in dark clothes. Peggy grabbed her *healing kit* — rosary beads, clipboard, a handful of business cards, and the battery candles from Wilko she used for ambience. Kevin pocketed a Mars Bar and said, "Look at us, Peg — Ghostbusters of Basildon. Who you gonna call? Us, apparently!" He chuckled, pleased with his joke.

She smirked despite herself. "Less talking, more haunting."

The hospital car park was half-empty, sodium lights flickering. Inside, the corridors were long, sterile, and somehow still sticky underfoot. As usual the hospital air smelled of disinfectant, tea, and tiredness.

A security guard at reception looked up as they entered. "Evenin'."

"Just a few prayers with the poorly ones," Peggy said sweetly, holding up a tin of biscuits. "For the staff, bless you," and she handed the tin to him. He grinned, then nodded. "All right, love. But don't go into the restricted wards."

"Wouldn't dream of it," she said, smiling, as Kevin pushed past her toward the lift.

The hospital ward was almost silent — save for the beeping of monitors and the soft hiss of machines. Peggy's heels clicked too loudly on the floor. She winced and swapped to a shuffle.

At the far end, a man lay motionless, tubes everywhere. She remembered him from last week — quiet family, nice wife, left her number on the prayer card.

Kevin checked the corridor. "Quickly, Peg. Before someone comes."

Peggy's voice trembled. "You sure we should—?"

"You said yourself," Kevin muttered. "He's ready. Spirit's knocking."

Her hands shook as she touched the edge of the machine. "If you're listening, love," she whispered, "go gentle, all right?"

She pressed a button.

The monitor's beep slowed… once, twice… then stopped. A long, low tone filled the room.

Peggy's chest clenched. She felt it before she heard it — a breath, soft but close, not from the bed behind her but from the corner of the room.

You took me too soon.

Peggy spun round.

No one there. Just the dim shape of wheelchair by the curtain, one wheel twitching ever so slightly.

"Kev?" she whispered.

Kevin was pale. "It's just static, Peg. Come on, let's go."

The light above them flickered. Then the bed creaked. The sheet moved.

Kevin swore under his breath. "Bloody hell—"

The machine's display blinked back to life — but the bed was empty.

They froze. For a second, the world seemed to hold its breath. Then, somewhere down the hall, an alarm began to wail.

"Run," said Peggy.

And they did.

They tore down the corridor, shoes squeaking, hearts hammering. The lift doors slid open before they pressed the button. Kevin shoved her in, panting.

"Don't say a word."

The lift descended with a groan. Peggy stared at the panel. Their reflections were faint in the steel. Behind her, for just a second, she thought she saw another figure — pale, eyes glassy, smiling faintly. Then gone.

Back home, the bungalow felt colder than when they'd left it. Peggy went straight to the sink, scrubbing her hands raw under the tap. The water ran pink against her nails. Kevin leaned on the counter, lighting a cigarette with shaking fingers.

"Well," he said, forcing a laugh, "that's another job well done."

She didn't answer. The tap dripped. Once. Twice. The sound was unbearable.

When she finally looked up, she saw her reflection in the kitchen window — tired, hollow-eyed. Kevin's reflection should've been beside her. But there was only hers.

"Kev?" she whispered.

He was still talking — something about the caravan, about money. But in the glass, there was only Peggy.

And just behind her reflection's shoulder, a faint, clouded face — smiling.

# Chapter
9

The Things That Move

Kevin Morpeth didn't believe in ghosts.

He believed in cash, caravans, and a decent fry-up. He believed in keeping the act smooth, the bookings steady, and the gin topped up for the emotional ones. But ghosts? No. That was Peggy's department.

Still, their home felt wrong that morning. Too still. Too clean. Even the kettle sounded suspicious, clicking like it was thinking about something.

Peggy was in the bedroom, still in her dressing gown, staring at her mirror as if it might tell her what she'd done. Kevin made tea — two sugars, extra strong — and tried to whistle. The sound came out thin and dry.

"You all right in there, love?" he called.

Silence.

He frowned. "Peg?"

A door creaked. Then her voice floated — soft, distracted. "Someone's been in the bathroom."

Kevin rolled his eyes. "No one's been in here, Peg. You're seeing things."

But when he went looked, the mirror over the sink was misted — even though there'd been no shower, no steam. And there, across the glass, faint but visible:

YOU TOOK ME TOO SOON.

Kevin stared. His mouth went dry.

"Bloody nonsense," he muttered. "Condensation trick, that's all."
He wiped it with his sleeve. The letters smeared — and then, slowly, reappeared beneath, clearer this time.

Peggy stood behind him in the doorway. "See?" she whispered. "They're not gone."

Kevin forced a laugh. "It's condensation. Spells anything if you stare long enough. Bit like your 'spirit board,' eh?"

He turned away too quickly.

By lunchtime, Peggy had retreated to the sofa, wrapped in her shawl, watching the telly without seeing it. A quiz show burbled cheerfully: *'Name a famous ghost'*

She switched it off.

Kevin tried to get on with his accounts — paper scattered across the table, biro tapping. But the numbers wouldn't stay still. A flicker, a shadow, and suddenly all the nines looked like sixes. He blinked, rubbed his eyes. The ink bled faintly into the paper, forming words.

You took me too soon.

He shoved the papers aside, heart thudding. "I'm losing it," he said aloud. "That's all. Bit of stress. Nothing a pint can't fix."

He stood — and the chair scraped backwards on its own.

Just a fraction.

Just enough to make his stomach twist.

That night, the sounds began.

Not the usual creaks and drips, but softer things — a whisper behind the curtains, the faint shuffle of slippers across the hall. Once, Kevin thought he heard a bed creak in the spare room, though it hadn't been used in months.

"Peg," he hissed. "You hearing this?"

She stirred beside him. "It's them."

"Oh, for—" He sat up, grabbing his phone torch. "There's no *them*. It's draughts and imagination."

But when he turned the light toward the doorway, the beam fell on a wheelchair. Their hallway was small, narrow — they didn't own a wheelchair. The thing sat still for a long second, metal gleaming dully.

Then one wheel twitched, like a slow nod.

Kevin dropped the phone. The light went out.

Something breathed beside his ear.

You took me too soon.

The next morning, Kevin looked wrecked — grey under the eyes, hands shaking as he buttered toast. Peggy just sat opposite him, calm now in a strange, hollow way. "They're getting closer," she said.

He snapped. "Stop it! There's no *they!* It's guilt, Peg. Conscience, that's all. You feel bad because we—" He stopped himself, too late.

"Because we what?" she asked softly.

The butter knife slipped from his hand and hit the floor with a sharp, metallic *clang*.

Outside, the bin lorry rumbled by. Inside, the air thickened. The kitchen clock ticked slower than it should.

Then came the sound again — faint at first, then stronger: The slow, rhythmic squeak of wheels on tile, coming from the hallway.

Peggy turned toward the sound, eyes wide but dry.

"Kevin," she whispered, "I think they've come to our home."

He swallowed hard. The toast popped up, cold and untouched. The kettle clicked off by itself.

Kevin forced a grin. "You know what, Peg? I think we need a little holiday. Bit of sea air. Clear our heads."

Peggy didn't look away from the doorway.
"I don't think we're the ones who need air, Kevin."

He followed her gaze — and for just a second, thought he saw movement. Not fast. Not frightening. Just… a quiet figure, crossing the hall.

Bare feet. Hospital gown. Pale as light.

Then it was gone.

The aroma of antiseptic and instant coffee filled the surgery. Peggy sat on the edge of the paper-covered couch, handbag clutched tight on her lap, while Dr. Malhotra tapped at his keyboard. The clock above the filing cabinet ticked too loudly.

He turned to her, smiling the polite, efficient smile of someone already thinking about their next patient.

"Nothing's wrong with you, Peggy. All your vitals are functioning as they should."

"Nothing?" she said. "You mean I'm absolutely healthy?"

"Well," he said, glancing at the notes, "apart from trying to lose a little weight."

"Cheeky!"

He raised his hands. "Just the facts. Your BMI could be a touch lower, that's all." He leaned back, the chair creaking. "But should anything happen to you now, you'd be the healthiest corpse in the morgue."

He chuckled at his own joke. Peggy managed a polite smile — until she realised he wasn't stopping. The chuckle deepened, warped, became something else — a thick, rattling laugh that filled the room. His mouth opened wider, and wider still, until it wasn't a mouth anymore but a great, black hole. A soundless cavern pulling everything towards it — the light, the air, her breath—

Then, suddenly, it was gone. Dr. Malhotra was back at his desk, pen in hand, smiling as if nothing had happened.

"Peggy? Is there anything else?"

Peggy blinked. Her throat was dry.
"No," she said quietly. "Nothing at all."

As she left the surgery, the corridor seemed longer than before. The posters on the walls — flu jab reminders, mental health helplines — all stared at her with too many eyes.

Outside, the air felt wrong again. He'd said she was healthy. But she knew — in her bones, in her breath — that something had started inside her. Something she couldn't explain.

Chapter 10

Voices on the Line

Peggy arrived home pale as candle wax, clutching the doctor's leaflet about "Managing Stress and Delusions."

Kevin was at the kitchen table, laptop open, crumbs on the keyboard, a half-eaten sausage roll resting on an unpaid gas bill. He didn't look up.

"Morning, Doctor Death," he said cheerfully. "How's the old ticker?"

Peggy dropped her handbag onto a chair. "Nothing wrong with me, apparently. 'Healthiest corpse in the morgue,' he said. Thought that was hilarious."

Kevin chuckled. "Good bedside manner, that. See? You're fine. Which means—"

She groaned. "Don't say it."

"Another booking! Got one lined up already. Saturday night. Twelve quid a head, tea included."

She stared at the screen. "We can't, Kev. Not after—"

He beamed. "Course we can! You'll show 'em you've still got the magic touch. Just do a little research like usual and you'll have them all believing there's a hereafter "

The Pretence of Normal

That afternoon, Peggy tried to act normal.

She polished the ornaments, folded laundry and fed the cat, although it had now moved in with a neighbour. The kettle whistled — and under the shriek she swore it said her name.

She wandered into the lounge, switched on the tv and slumped into a chair. During an advert break the television murmured something about funeral plans, and a voice beneath it whispering, *"She took us..."*

She pressed her palms to her ears. "Get a grip, Peg," she muttered. "You're not losing it. You can't afford to."

By six o'clock Kevin had loaded the van. "All right, Miss Mystic? Let's show the spirits who's boss."

She clutched her notebook like a hymn book. "If we must."

The Show Must Go On

The hall was small and beige — all community halls in Essex are. Four dozen people sat in rows, each with a polystyrene cup of tea. A poster behind her read:

"PEGGY MORPETH — Medium to the Stars (and the Rest of Us)."

Printed by Kevin in Comic Sans.

Peggy took the mic. "Evening, loves. The spirit world's queueing up tonight — can't resist a good raffle prize."

Polite laughter. Weak, but serviceable. She smiled, slipping into her rhythm. "Now then, I've a gentleman here, says his name's—"

The microphone fizzed. Then, before she spoke again, a low voice came through the speakers.

"She took us."

A beat of silence.

Then an old man at the back chuckled. "Bit harsh, innit?"

Laughter, nervous but real.

Kevin, sweating at the edge of the stage, hissed, "Keep going, Peg!"

She forced a grin. "Spirits, eh? Some of them are right comedians"

A few giggles. She pressed on. "Right, now I've a lady with me. Sweet woman, bit of chest trouble, passed in hospital—"

Her voice cracked mid-sentence. Deeper now. Slower. Her next word came out in a voice not her own — slower, rasping, male

"Graham Tilley. Ward C. Tuesday night."

A woman's cry cut through the room. "That's my brother! Went sooner than we thought!"

"No, love his time had come……." Peggy's face then dropped into a deep frown and again the raspy claimed, "She did it, turned off my machine"

Peggy's mouth trembled. "No — I mean, yes, he says—"

Her words twisted, the tone no longer hers.
"We didn't need you. Now you have us."

The urn in the corner hissed, boiling over.
Kevin darted forward. "Technical glitch! Just a bit of feedback, folks—"

But Peggy's eyes rolled back. The microphone crackled, and a chorus of voices burst through, overlapping, broken, desperate.

"You took us."
"It wasn't our time."

Peggy's head was thrashing from side to side, her tongue twisting around in her mouth, dribble rolling down her chin. Her body trembling.

The room darkened. The lights flickered like old film stock.

Peggy's body shock savagely, then she walked, zombie-like across the stage and pointed at a man in the audience **"Dave, save them, save the rest, don't let her turn off their life support!"**

A chair toppled; someone screamed. The smell of hot metal filled the air.

Peggy stumbled and fell lifeless to the stage.

Kevin grabbed the mic. "No refunds!" he barked, panicking.

Then the lights went out entirely.

There were screams, the sound of plastic chairs scraping across the floor, and the sound of hurried footsteps leaving the hall. The doors swung open and clattered back on themselves again and again, as if pushed by a frantic, invisible crowd long after the living had already escaped.

When the lights returned, Peggy was sitting upright in a chair, eyes wide and distant, her hands bleeding from clenched fists. The audience had halved. Those who remained clutched their phones, screens glowing, recording.

Kevin helped her up, muttering, "You're fine, love, just nerves—"

She looked past him, to the far wall. A pale reflection shimmered in the varnished wood — rows of faces, hollow-eyed, mouths open but silent.

Then it was gone.

The Drive Home.

Rain lashed the van windscreen. Kevin sat behind the wheel, shaking, trying to sound casual. "You've gone viral, Peg. You'll be on telly by Tuesday."

The wipers scraped once, twice, then stopped mid-sweep."

She didn't look at him. "They won't stop now, Kev. They're not finished."

He forced a laugh. "You're scaring yourself."
But as he reached for the ignition, the van's radio crackled on by itself.

From the speakers came her own voice — low, hollow, and certain:

"You took us!"

Kevin switched it off, but the echo hung in the silence like smoke. Outside the car park lights flickered — once, twice — then steadied, as if nothing had happened.

Peggy sat rigid, staring through the glass.

In the windscreen's reflection, three faint faces hovered behind them — pale, patient, waiting.

Chapter 11

The Aftermath.

The morning after the séance, the Morpeths' bungalow looked like the aftermath of a charity sale. Cups everywhere, curtains half-drawn, and Kevin glued to his phone like a teenager. The headline flashed on every feed:

"Basildon Medium Becomes Possessed Live on Stage!"

The clip had thousands of views already — shaky footage of Peggy on stage, voice shifting, eyes rolled back. Commenters argued in the thread below.

"Genuine mediumship!"
"Fake as a fiver from Wish."
"That voice though 😨 😨 😨"

Kevin couldn't look away. Half-proud, half-horrified. "Your face is plastered across every feed, Peg," he said, almost reverent. "Proper local celebrity, you are."

Peggy sat in her dressing gown, a half-drunk tea cooling in her hands. The phone rang again — reporters, fans, sceptics, maybe the police. She didn't answer. Her hands were shaking.

"I don't want to be famous," she said quietly.

Kevin grinned without looking up. "It's not about fame, love. It's about business. We can finally afford that new caravan I showed you — maybe even the deluxe one, with the skylight."

She stared at him. "You didn't see what I saw, Kev."

He finally looked up, eyes bright. "I saw pound signs, Peg. Bright ones."

Her voice hardened. "You're not listening."

"I'm listening just fine," he snapped. "I'm listening to opportunity knocking, that's what I'm listening to. You and your nerves — we've got bookings waiting, people begging to see you, and you're sat there like someone's died."

Peggy looked at him for a long moment. "Someone has, Kev."

He rolled his eyes and reached for another sausage roll.

By that afternoon, the bungalow had changed. Not visibly — no broken windows or toppled chairs — but in its temperature, its mood. The toilet hissed when no one was near it. "The bathroom light flickered as Peggy washed her hands. The tap sputtered, then stopped dead. On the tiled wall above the sink, water streaks ran upward instead of down — shaping, for just a second, into two crooked words:

TOO SOON.

She blinked, and the pattern was gone. Just damp tiles.

Her heart thudded. "It's the plumbing," she whispered. "Just the bloody plumbing." You've got overactive imagination, that's your problem." She mumbled to herself.

But later that night, she heard it again — a faint hospital beep under the hum of the fridge. She pressed her ear to the wall. The sound was inside it, pulsing, rhythmic.

Kevin couldn't hear a thing.

By Wednesday, they had company. Two teenage girls with phones stood at the garden gate filming interent videos, shouting through the hedge.

"Who killed Graham Tilley!" one of them sang, doing a mock séance dance. Kevin stormed out in his vest and slippers, waving a broom.

"Go on, clear off before I call the police!"

They ran off laughing.

Peggy watched from the window, pale as milk. "It's not funny, Kev."

He was red-faced and puffing. "Course it's not funny. They're making a mockery of you, that's all. Jealous little cows."

But he looked shaken when he came back inside. For the first time, he locked the door behind him.

That evening, Peggy had had enough. She packed a small suitcase — pyjamas, cash, her diary — and set it by the door. She wasn't just leaving the house. She was leaving Kevin, the séances, all of it.

When she turned the handle, a sharp tone filled the hallway.

Flat. Endless.

Like a heart monitor flatlining.

Peggy froze. The sound came from nowhere and everywhere. She let go of the handle. The tone stopped instantly. She turned slowly down the hallway. The air was thick — not cold, just heavy, like something holding its breath.

And then she saw them.

Figures, faint at first, gathering in the half-light — hospital gowns hanging loose, feet bare on the laminate floor. Their faces were pale, waxy, eyes unfocused, as though they hadn't quite remembered how to look at her.

The beeping started again — slow, steady, growing louder with every step they took. Peggy backed away, shaking her head.

"Not now," she whispered. "Please, not now."

But the sound built to a solid, choking rhythm — the pulse of machines, of endings — until it filled the house like breath.

And then, as suddenly as it came, it stopped.

She whispered, "They won't let me go."

Kevin sat in the living room later, the telly flickering weakly. He'd had enough of her moods. "You're losing it, Peg," he muttered. "It's guilt or hormones or both."

He turned up the volume. The picture wavered — static, then a corridor. A hospital corridor, stretching out of sight. Fluorescent lights buzzed. Through the glass doors at the end, he saw his own reflection staring back.

Behind him, something exhaled. He turned sharply. Nothing there.

"Peg?" he called.

Silence. Then a voice, quiet, close:

"Your turn."

Kevin clutched his chest. The air thickened, pressing down. His breath came short and ragged. He slumped back into the chair, gasping, as the static on the telly fizzed into a laugh — long, low, and wrong.

Peggy woke in the dark. The bed was cold. Kevin wasn't there. From the hallway came the flicker of light, and a sound — laughter, distorted, familiar.

She crept to the living room. The television glowed pale blue. Kevin sat slumped forward in the armchair, the back of his head visible in the screen's reflection.

On the TV, a live image played — the same room, same chair. The two of them, shown from somewhere unseen. Peggy blinked. In the broadcast, Kevin's reflection turned, slowly, and looked straight at her.

"Kevin?" she whispered.

He didn't move.

She hurried round to the front of the chair.

His face was grey, still, eyes open.

Peggy screamed.

The Hospital

Machines beeped steadily. Kevin lay motionless beneath the sheet, a breathing tube taped to his mouth. Peggy sat at his side, hands clasped tight in her lap.

The nurse had said he might recover. But Peggy wasn't sure she wanted him to.

She thought of the séances, the greed, the voices. The faces in the dark. How he'd pushed and pushed until she could barely breathe.

The monitor's beeps matched her pulse.

One, two, three.

She reached out, fingers hovering over the switch.

"If I do this," she whispered, "maybe you'll stop haunting me too."

And she pressed it.

The machine wailed — a flat, final tone.

Peggy stood, breathing shallowly, and whispered into the silence:

"You were right, Kev. We're all going to the same place, although some a bit earlier than others".

Chapter 12

Drawer Next Door

The bungalow felt too quiet when Peggy came home. Not peaceful — hollow. The sort of quiet that listened back. A listening silence. A waiting silence. She shut the door behind her and stood for a moment in the hallway, waiting for the hum of the fridge, the tick of the kitchen clock. Nothing.

Just silence, thick enough that it felt like fog. On the doormat: condolence cards already.

So sorry for your loss.

Thinking of you,

Kev was a diamond.

She toed them aside, as though they were dust. She didn't want sympathy. She didn't want pity. She wanted sound — something real, something human. Kevin's phone was still on the counter, screen lighting up every few minutes: missed calls, voicemails, numbers she didn't recognise. Journalists, probably.

She picked it up once, thumbed over the screen, thought about answering, then set it down again.

The silence pressed closer. In the quiet, she realised she could still hear it —

the life-support beep.

Faint. Steady. Impossible.

Beep. Beep. Beep.

She unplugged the kettle, the clock, even the fridge. She pulled their plugs like a woman exorcising demons. The sound didn't stop. It just sank deeper into the house, as if it had found a place to live there. She backed into the lounge, heart hammering, clutching her dressing gown around herself like armour.

The house felt like it was breathing.

The police came the next afternoon.

A polite young detective with tired eyes and a clipboard, the kind that looked like he'd rather be anywhere else.

"Just routine, Mrs Morpeth," he said, perching on the edge of the sofa.

"Hospitals flagged a bit of an anomaly with your husband's file."

"Anomaly?" Peggy asked. Her voice came out thin.

He checked his notes. "The life-support machine. Someone interfered with the settings. No sign of forced entry, nothing violent. It's probably just a fault. But we have to tick every box."

Peggy smiled faintly, the same sweet, unbothered smile she used on stage.

"I wouldn't know the first thing about hospital machines, Detective. I get dizzy just looking at a plug socket."

He chuckled awkwardly, satisfied enough to stand. "Course. Sorry to intrude."

At the door, though, he hesitated.

"Strange thing, though — Kevin's monitor stopped at 3:33 a.m. That's the exact minute you signed the discharge papers."

Peggy blinked. "Is that right?"

He nodded, almost sheepish. "Coincidence, probably."

Then he left, shutting the door softly behind him. Peggy closed her eyes. The silence tightened around her like a fist.

Then — very faint —

Beep.

Beep.

Beep.

She clamped her hands over her ears.

It didn't help.

That night, she tried the radio for company. Some late-night call-in show, the kind Kevin used to fall asleep to. But the signal hissed, then warped. Through the static, a voice she knew too well crackled to life.

"Peg…"

Her throat closed.

"Peg, we could have been rich."

She hurled the radio across the room.

It cracked against the skirting board — but the voice went on, tinny and calm, as though the radio wasn't needed.

"Don't pretend you didn't enjoy it, Peg. You always loved the attention."

She pressed her palms over her ears. The sound was inside them now. The bungalow pulsed with it — like a living heart.

The next morning, she drew the curtains — and froze. Figures stood on the lawn. Dozens of them. Pale, thin, wearing hospital gowns that fluttered in the wind. Their faces half-lit, their eyes hollow.

She knew them all.

Every name she'd ever spoken on stage. Everyone she'd ever "summoned." At the front, a man with thinning grey hair and a bandaged hand raised his chin.

"Graham Tilley," she whispered.

He smiled faintly and mouthed,

"You killed us".

Then, behind him — Kevin. Just standing there, watching. Peggy stumbled back, heart thudding. She slammed the curtains shut, hands trembling so hard the fabric slipped through her fingers.

The room darkened again.

But she could feel the eyes outside.

Waiting.

Watching.

By evening, she'd stopped eating.

The kettle was still unplugged, the telly off, every mirror turned to the wall. She muttered to herself — half prayers, half bargains, insisting she meant no harm, that she only wanted to help.

The silence soaked up every word.

Neighbours said later they heard her pacing, heard the fridge door open and close, open and close, like she was checking for someone inside.

Checking for him.

Checking for them.

When the police finally forced the door (alerted by a neighbour who "smelled something off"), they found her collapsed in the hallway.

Cold, breathing faintly, eyes open but seeing nothing.

Her lips parted. They said she whispered as they lifted her onto the stretcher.

Something about drawers.

The ambulance lights flashed down the road, siren low. Peggy stirred once, eyes fluttering open. Inside the hum and rattle of the van, she heard a voice by her ear — soft, familiar, smug.

"Don't worry, love," Kevin said.

"You'll be with me soon. Drawer next door."

Chapter 13

The Healthiest Corpse in the Morgue

Peggy woke to cold. The kind that seeped straight through skin and bone. She couldn't move her arms. Couldn't breathe properly. Metal against her shoulders, her knees.

She tried to lift a hand. It thudded against steel inches above her face.

No room. No space. No air.

Her breath bounced back at her, warm and wet, gathering into little clouds of condensation she could smell — stale, sour, recycled.

Her teeth shuddered.

For a moment she thought she was dreaming — until she smelled disinfectant and something sweeter underneath. A scent she recognised from hospital wards — decomposing roses.

Then she realised where she was.

The drawer.
The morgue.

Time ceased to exist. Minutes or hours passed. Impossible to know. Her breath rasped. Her pulse thudded in her ears like footsteps coming nearer.

A sound: metal creaked. Another drawer sliding open.

Peggy stopped breathing.

Kevin's voice drifted out, casual as ever, as though he were leaning from a pub stool.
"Didn't have to do it, Peg. Could've made a fortune, me and you. The telly, the tours…"

His voice softened, dropping to a wheezy whisper.
"Still — you always had to have the last word, didn't you?"

Peggy forced her voice through the tightness in her throat.
"Kevin?"

Silence.

Then — laughter. Not just his. Others. Layers of voices, overlapping like tangled bedsheets.

She recognised the cadence of Graham's laugh. The gasping misery of Angela Fuller. The little cough of Mr Ingram who died on Ward C.

She had stolen their stories. Pretended their voices came from light. From angels.

Now they came from the dark.

Names whispered. Dates. Wards. Rooms. Last breaths. Failing hearts. Morphine they begged for.

One voice sobbed, "Help me, Peg."
Another hissed, "You left me alone."
A third chuckled, "Now we're all together."

Peggy hammered the metal. Her nails tore and bled. Her breath came in ragged bursts. Her own voice broke into small, miserable noises.

The drawer walls carried every vibration — her cries shaking back at her like someone else screaming with her.

Peggy hammered the metal. Her nails tore and bled. Her breath came in ragged bursts. Her own voice broke into small, miserable noises.

She tried to draw her knees up — impossible. She tried to turn — impossible. The metal pressed her shoulders like a coffin's embrace. Cold. Tight. Final.

"Kevin… Kevin, you've got to help me," she sobbed, her teeth rattling. "I shouldn't be in here. There's nothing wrong with me. I'm not dead. Kevin… *please*."

The laughter returned, layered and mocking, like a bad choir singing slightly out of tune.

"She thought she was special…"
"Thought she could trick the dead…"
"She didn't hear us scream…"
"Now she screams instead…"

Peggy pressed her forehead against the steel until the pain blurred her thoughts. "Stop it. *Stop it.* I only wanted to help. I only ever tried to help people."

A voice hissed through the dark:
"No. You helped yourself."

Another voice answered with a wet, gurgling rasp:
"You never spoke to us — you stole from us."

Peggy shook her head fiercely. "That's not true! Kevin— tell them, tell them I didn't mean it—"

Kevin's chuckle slid through the freezing space like oil.

"Oh, Peg… you meant every bit of it. You loved the attention. Loved knowing things no one else did. Loved being the star."

The whispering spirits laughed harder, overlapping, mocking:

"Could've been rich…"
"She chose the applause…"
"She liked the spotlight…"
"Now she's in the dark…"

Peggy's shoulders shook violently. "Kevin— please— I can't stay here. I can't. I'm not dead! I'm breathing, I'm talking, I'm—"

Kevin's voice drifted closer, almost tender.

"That's the best bit."

Peggy froze, breath shallow, heart stuttering.

Then Kevin's voice came again, lazy and pleased.

"The healthiest corpse in the morgue."

Epilogue.

Essex Gazette – page 6.

Human Interest.

"Tragic Coincidence at an Essex Mortuary"

Hospital officials have confirmed a "rare refrigeration error" after a woman was found *alive* inside a mortuary drawer at an Essex hospital.

Mrs Peggy Morpeth, 59, of Laindon, had been admitted for observation following the sudden death of her husband, local entrepreneur, Kevin Morpeth.

Staff were said to be "shocked but relieved" that Mrs Morpeth appeared "remarkably healthy" despite her ordeal.

A hospital spokesperson described her recovery as "nothing short of miraculous," adding that Mrs Morpeth is "helping police with their enquiries into technical issues affecting several life-support machines across Essex hospitals."

When pressed for further comment, the spokesperson smiled awkwardly and said only:

"She's in stable condition — the healthiest corpse we've ever seen."

The End.

The Dolls House Players

Chapter 1

Wendy

Wendy stood on-set just behind the camera. She could feel every tiny hair on her body standing to attention, and small beads of sweat trickling down the back of her neck.

This wasn't fear, or nerves, or an indication of doubt — it was excitement.

Pure, fizzing excitement.

She was born for this. Standing in the director's eyeline, mic'ed up, hair and makeup set just so.

Ready.

She straightened her shoulders and lifted her chin, the lights bouncing off her freshly powdered skin. Wendy loved this part — the quiet seconds before the action. The way everything held its breath. The promise that she was about to be somebody else.

"Rolling… action!" The director called.

Her pulse quickened.

Almost.

Waiting.

On-set, the other actors were already mid-performance a conversation — back and forth, back and forth — seamless, polished, like they'd been born on a camera.

Wendy checked for her mark. There it was: a square of blue tape on the studio floor, just beyond the broken-down car prop in the garage set.

Any minute now…

She stepped onto the set. The director looked up, gave her a tiny nod — her cue.

Now.

"How much you charging me to fix this bleedin' thing?!" She'd delivered her line.

A snap of silence.

Then—

"Cut!"

The director leaned forward, pleasant but firm. "Wendy darling, that was good. I loved the way you glided into the scene, but there's no bleedin' in the script."

"Oh, blimey! Excuse me, did I say that again? Must be me nerves. Sorry."

She felt every molecule of embarrassment gather in her cheeks.

"Re-set... take 3, from the top," called the director.

Wendy retreated to her off-set spot in the dark corners of the garage, shaking her head at herself. Why did she do that? Why did she always improvise when she got excited? She had to keep herself in-check. One more mishap and she could be out. She pinched her own wrist — a tiny sting, punishment enough.

"Rolling... action."

This time, when Wendy hit her mark, it was perfect.

She delivered her line with character and confidence, catching the other actor's eyeline like she'd been taught, reacting to the tiny flicker of disapproval he gave her, transforming it into playful defiance.

She lived the line, not just said it.

She was a born natural.

And she knew it. Acting wasn't just pretending. Acting was breathing somebody else's air.

She was going places — she could feel it. Pinewood, Elstree, maybe even Hollywood — why not? Dreams had to start somewhere.

But she needed more lines. Bigger parts. She needed someone who believed in her. She'd have to speak to Sid. Sid — her agent — who never seemed to send her to the right auditions. Who didn't have the right contacts. Whose idea of "networking" was sharing a Greggs sausage roll with a retired camera operator.

Maybe she should drop him? Maybe she needed one of those flash West End agents.

But Sid had been good to her, hadn't he? He'd got her the featured roles, even if he'd bungled a few introductions. Sid was loyal, but loyalty didn't book jobs. She glanced down at herself, smoothing the wrinkles in her costume. She was plump — not fat, no — just pleasingly built. A proper figure. Busty, curvy, the kind of woman who stood her ground physically and emotionally. People listened when she walked into a room. She had a bright smile that made strangers trust her, and she never let anything dampen her spirit.

Her brown hair framed her heart-shaped face beautifully, her hazel eyes softening at the corners. Warm eyes, the sort that made you think she had a secret kindness tucked away.

She had never trained properly in drama — no Mountview, no RADA — just extras work and a few lucky breaks where directors liked her natural attitude.

A cockney accent came naturally — even though she was from Essex, not London, so she wasn't exactly a real Cockney. But she could fake it well enough to fool most. East End banter was her superpower. She was a little dramatic, a touch too talkative, and a tad nosy — but she had heart.

And that heartbeat for acting.

Suddenly, Wendy noticed the lead actor staring at her — evaluating her, almost impressed, she hoped. The director turned toward her again, eyebrows raised.

"Wendy, love, that was spot on. Keep it like that."

She nodded, cheeks warm. "Promise."

The camera was reset. The director busied himself. Makeup stepped in with a puff of powder on someone's forehead. A stagehand adjusted a loose wire near the car bonnet.

Wendy stepped back beside the camera and tried to swallow the tremor of excitement bubbling up. She'd done well today, she'd been seen. Noticed.

Maybe after this job, she'd have that chat with Sid over a cuppa and demand bigger roles. Demand something with lines. Demand something that proved she was more than a body in the background.

Chapter 2

Seaside.

Torquay, Devon — Summer

Torquay was glittering. The sun struck the wet sand until it shone like tin foil, gulls screamed above the smell of frying oil, and the air shimmered with sugar. Candyfloss spun in pink clouds, children ran with dripping ice creams, and the sound of the fairground organ chased the tide back and forth.

On the promenade, a small striped tent had drawn a crowd. Mothers leaned on pushchairs, fathers squinted in the glare, and children pressed close to the wooden booth where Mr Punch was giving his famous laugh.

"Now that's the way to do it!" he shrieked, stick in hand, as Judy wagged her finger at him. The children roared. A baby howled in confusion.

From a distance, it looked like any seaside show — bright, noisy, harmless. But up close, the strings on their painted hands were so fine they caught the sunlight like spider silk, almost invisible. The puppeteer's hands jerked and danced behind the curtain, yet sometimes the figures seemed to move before he did, as though anticipating the pull.

The crowd didn't notice. They never did.

The puppeteer, a man of indeterminate middle age with a small comb-over and a sunburnt neck, worked the booth with the precision of a surgeon with the cheer of a condemned man.

Every so often he would look up and glance at the crowd. His eyes like tiny black beads searching faces, like a hunter looking for prey.

"Give us a kiss!" Punch crowed, his squeaky voice rising above the gulls. The crowd laughed. Judy came up swinging her rolling pin, and Punch, ever the gentleman, returned the favour with his stick. The children howled their approval. Parents smiled cheerfully. The baby puppet cried with theatrical distress before Punch cheerfully hurled it out of sight.

Everything as it should be.

Almost.

The show ended to applause, a small tin bucket filling with coins. Mr Larkin, the puppeteer, bowed stiffly, thanked the crowd, and pulled the curtain shut.

Inside the booth, the air was hot, close, and faintly scented with salt and wood varnish. He wiped his face and set Punch and Judy on the small bench in the makeshift stage. Their painted smiles gleamed in the dimness.

"Good show," he muttered to no one in particular and headed off to the pavilion opposite for a cool pint.

The red velvet stage curtains were now closed. A gold cord keeping them together. Backstage the lights were dim smell of greasepaint hung in the air. The atmosphere was electric, an outstanding performance, worthy of an Oscar. The crowd's applause was still ringing in the actors' ears, and they are still high on adrenaline, well one of them at least…..

"I was born to be on stage, it's in my blood, my bones. I eat and drink the theatre!" Brian, still in his Punch outfit proclaimed. He look around him . The excitement wasn't shared.

"Come on you lot! What's got into you, it's the best job in the World and we're good at it" Brian urged.

A moment passed. Then, very softly, Judy's head turned toward him. "If you hit me with that blooming stick again," she said, voice low and sharp, "I'll give you a wallop you won't forget."

Brian blinked once, his painted grin unmoving. "It's part of the act," he said. "They expect it. It's in the script."

"Well, next time," she hissed, "be a bit more gentle "

Brian rolled his eyes, a laugh half-born in his throat. "It's got to look authentic love, we're professionals. I have a reputation to withhold".

"You're an idiot Brian! The only prize you'll get is for being that! This life, I don't want it. I want to be a normal woman again, I want grandchildren, holidays in France. I don't want to be a poor excuse for a puppet. I don't want to be a quarter of the size I should be!" Tears welled in her throat and she fled the stage.

"Always had a theatrical temperament that one", Brian mumbled to himself.

Outside, the last of the daylight died. The sound of the sea grew louder, and seagulls scavenged around on the sand for what had been left behind.

The wallpaper was enormous. Roses the size of dinner plates climbed the walls, their petals a frozen bloom of glossed paint, their stems thick as pipes twisting skyward. A small brass clock, ticking cheerfully, loomed over the mantelpiece like a tower guarding a tiny civilisation. Apart from these little oddities, the house was beautiful. Brian loved it. A replica of a double-fronted 1930's family home — neatly symmetrical, lovingly detailed, perfectly polished. A home any successful actor would be proud of, he always said, even though the hallway light was as large as a harvest moon and the banister posts were wide enough to lean a whole body against.

Judy dropped her painted smile and rubbed her jaw.

"Honestly," she said, "you could have aimed lower with that stick. My ear's ringing."

Brian grinned — or at least, his face managed the fixed, manic shape of one. The paint around his mouth cracked ever so slightly, a reminder that their expressions were not entirely their own anymore.

"It's stagecraft, darling. Precision. You've got to give the audience energy." He adjusted his crimson cap, tugging it into place as though preparing to greet a West End audience. He looked around their house with managerial pride, hands behind his back as he surveyed the room like a director inspecting a set. To him, it was showbiz magic — a place of rehearsals, routines, purpose.

To Judy, it was a prison built from mahogany and spite.

On the kitchen counter, enormous mushrooms lay like fallen trees. Judy was chopping one with a knife the size of a sword, muttering as she wrestled the blade through its soft trunk.

"You and your energy. One of these days, I'll give you a burst of it, see how you like it."

From the sitting room came the sound of lazy chatter — the background artists, as Brian called them. Two chorus girls and an old man who'd once been in a toothpaste commercial. They were lounging on matchbox sofas, legs dangling over the sides, arguing about who'd had the better agent in their former lives.

"I had a BBC casting once," one of the chorus girls said proudly.

"You were shortlisted," the other corrected. "I actually filmed something."

The old man harrumphed. "Agents, the lot of them, vultures in suits. Mine said I had 'range'. Look where it got me — on a sofa made of cardboard and shame."

Brian clapped his hands. The sound was sharp, theatrical, and echoed like thunder in their shrunken world.

"Team meeting in five! We've got a matinee tomorrow and I want spirit! Real spark!"

The old man groaned.

"We're puppets, Brian. Spirit's what got us here."

But Brian barely heard him — or perhaps he chose not to. He was pacing already, full of purpose, the eternal ham even in captivity. He adjusted imaginary cuffs, straightened his waistcoat, practised a bow to an invisible crowd.

"Failure's a choice," he declared, puffing out his chest. "Look at us now — top billing at Torquay! The kids love us. We're alive again!"

Judy slammed her knife into the chopping board. The floor trembled beneath them, plates rattling faintly in the cupboard as though the house itself flinched.

"Alive?" she said. "We're miniature. We sleep in a doll's house. And the man who did this to us — he pulls all the strings."

Her voice softened at the end, not with fear but with a fury she was too tired to raise any higher. For a moment, they both looked up.

Through the lace-curtained window, the shadow of the puppeteer moved past — slow, deliberate, godlike. A silhouette with long arms and an ever-present hum, as though he breathed the house into being with every pass. His footsteps reverberated through the wooden floor like distant thunder.

Brian straightened his waistcoat again, oddly reverent.

"He's given us purpose," he said.

Judy's laugh was thin and dangerous, echoing off the oversized walls.

"He's given us company. That's what you do with pets, Brian. You keep them because they clap when you feed them."

The background artists fell silent at that — even the chorus girls stopped bickering. It wasn't often Judy spoke with that tone, that quiet finality. It caught everyone by the collar.

The clock ticked. Each second sounded like a hammer strike.

Somewhere far above, the puppeteer began to whistle the Punch and Judy theme — jaunty, shrill, unending. It seeped into the house like damp. It always did.

Brian tried to smile again, but the paint at his cheeks felt stiff.

"Showtime tomorrow," he murmured. "We must be ready."

Judy looked at her reflection in the polished knife. Her painted eyes stared back — wide, bright, unblinking. A face made for entertainment, not expression.

"One day," she whispered.

And for the first time, even Brian felt the tremor beneath those words.

Chapter 3

Wendy

The shoot wrapped early that afternoon. Wendy peeled off her costume jacket, swapped her heels for trainers, and left the film location with a spring in her step that didn't quite hide her nerves. She loved acting with every beat of her heart — but love alone didn't keep an actress alive in this business.

The café near Torquays theatre — The Copper Kettle — was half-full. Warm steam fogged the windows. The smell of frying bacon and coffee beans clung to the air. Wendy chose a table tucked into the corner where she could see the door and not be seen too easily herself.

She ordered a veggie panini and a cup of tea. She never ate before filming — nerves knotted her stomach — but now she devoured the first half of the hot sandwich like a woman who'd survived a national famine.

Sid arrived six minutes late. For Sid, this was practically early.

"Wend!" He boomed, flustered and red-faced, squeezing himself between chairs as if the room had shrunk just to spite him. "Sorry, traffic was murder. I've been up and down that A3022 like a yo-yo all morning."

Wendy sipped her tea without looking up. "A sorry I'm late will do next time, Sid. Don't need the autobiography."

Sid blinked. "Bloody 'ell, someone's spiky today."

"Just direct," she corrected. "Didn't get much sleep. The agency needs to step up. I can't keep doing featured lines once every six months."

Sid gave a slow shrug, smoothing his moustache as if it held the secrets of the universe. "Work's work, Wend," he said, cautiously. "Everyone starts with scraps. You're lucky to even get scraps."

"I'm not lucky," Wendy replied. "I'm talented."

She leaned forward.

"I hit my mark every single take today. The director complimented me. You know what they're filming next month? A four-part drama. They're bringing in BBC writers — proper stuff. I could get a speaking role. They like me there. They use me. They trust me. I want to audition."

Sid twitched.

"Auditions…" he muttered, like a dog reacting to the word bath. "Now, Wend, they've got trained actors queuing for that. Someone from RADA, LAMDA, drama schools—"

"I don't care about drama schools," Wendy said. "They don't make people talented. They just make them posh. You've seen me. You know what I can do."

Sid shifted, uncomfortable. He fiddled with a sugar sachet and avoided her eyes. "Look," he tried, gently, "I don't want to see you get hurt. You're good, Wend — proper good — but you're not one of the golden names. Yet. We've got to play the game. A few more featured roles, a few continuity jobs, a—"

"I'm not waiting three bloody years!" Wendy's voice jolted the air between them. Then she lowered it, embarrassed but determined. "I'm ready now, Sid. If you don't push me, I'll find someone who will."

That sentence hung between them like a pulled trigger.

Sid actually looked wounded. "You'd leave me?"

"Not if you prove you believe in me," Wendy replied. "But I need something real, something meaty. Lines. Character. Depth. I didn't come this far just to be 'woman at bus stop number three.'"

Sid frowned into his tea, as if answers might rise to the surface like steam.

"You want a lead?" He muttered.

"Eventually," Wendy said. "But right now? I'll take a decent supporting part. Someone with emotional range. Not just reacting to a lead actor's eyebrows."

There was silence.

Then Sid laughed — not mockingly, but with disbelief.

"You're a dark horse, Wend. Didn't know you had this fire in you."

"I've got more than fire," she said softly. "I've got purpose."

The waitress interrupted to refill their cups. Sid cleared his throat. "Right. I'll see what I can do. No promises, but… I'll try."

Wendy nodded, sitting taller. She believed him. She wanted to believe him.

She needed to.

They sat a moment in companionable silence. Sid fiddled with his napkin. Wendy wiped her lipstick from her cup. There was something electric building beneath the air, though neither understood it yet — that shift in atmosphere that comes before a storm, or a revelation, or a danger.

And then—

The bell above the café door chimed.

A man walked in.

He didn't belong there, not among the chintz curtains and chipped mugs. Tall, immaculate, dressed in charcoal and velvet, with the faintest scent of expensive cologne — old theatre, smoke, spices from another time. He moved with the ease of someone who expected space to be made for him. Wendy didn't know him; she hadn't seen him before.

But her heartbeat changed pace. The man looked towards their table.

And his eyes found Wendy.

Chapter 4

The New Actress

The dressing room shimmered faintly under the stage lights that filtered through the slats. The smell of singed fabric and greasepaint hung in the air. Tiny costumes—sequins, feathers, and miniature hats—lay draped over a thimble-sized ironing board. In the corner, the dolls' house clock struck nine, its chime a polite ding barely audible over the hum of the stage machinery above.

The puppeteer leaned down at the little wooden table. He was a tall man in a wine-red suit with brass buttons that glinted when he moved. His hair, slicked back with something that smelled faintly of oranges and oil, caught the light like lacquer. In his presence, even the air seemed to perform.

Brian stood proudly at attention beside Judy, who was making a performance of indifference—arms crossed, face set. The three background artists, hunched and half-asleep, occupied the tiny sofa like decorative props.

Patrick Larkin spread his hands in a gesture that was half blessing, half threat.

"My darlings," he announced, "I am no longer Patrick the Puppeteer but now—Valentino the Showman!

"The time has come to evolve. We've dazzled the seaside. We've conquered Torquay's toddlers and terrified the pensioners. But I—" he tapped his chest dramatically—"I dream bigger. We're moving on. England, Europe, the World! We're not just Punch and Judy. I'm talking Miller, Pinter… perhaps even Shakespeare!"

Brian's eyes gleamed. "At last!" he said, his voice bright with delight. "Serious theatre! Proper dialogue, projection, tragedy! I can see it now—Punch as Hamlet!"

"Punch as a ham," Judy muttered. "You'll be doing King Lear to seagulls."

Valentino's smile froze for a fraction of a second. Then it returned, tighter, toothier.

"Ah, Judy, the cynic's curse—she who cannot dream." He paced, boots echoing like timpani against the floor. "I want team players, Judy. If you're not happy, you can always sell ice cream." His laugh came out sudden and sharp, like a ventriloquist's crackle.

The background artists sniggered weakly, unsure whether to laugh or hide.

Valentino's eyes gleamed. "We need class. Refinement. A real lady to elevate our art. That's what we're missing."

Brian nodded eagerly, like a student desperate to please. "A leading lady—yes, yes, someone sophisticated. A touch of elegance!"

Judy's voice was flat. "Someone to make me look common, you mean."

Valentino ignored her, gazing upward as though addressing a celestial audience. "A proper actress," he murmured. "Poised. Graceful. The sort of woman who knows her forks."

That evening, down on the Torquay promenade, the smell of vinegar and sugar hung thick in the air. The fairground lights blinked red and blue across the windows of a small café with a flickering sign that read Seaview Snacks. The sea was only visible as a bruised shimmer behind the rides.

Inside, Wendy sat slouched in a plastic booth, stirring tea gone cold. Her lipstick had worn to a faint smudge, and the corners of her eyes showed the kind of exhaustion that comes from too many auditions and not enough parts. Across from her sat her agent, Sid—anxious, sallow, and habitually damp, as if he'd been sweating since 1973.

"You need to up your game, Wendy," Sid was saying, tapping a greasy finger on the table. "No one's casting female cockneys these days—it's all posh birds. Posh birds and drama school types."

"Posh birds?" she said, her accent thick as syrup. "I can do posh." She straightened her back and, in a crisp, perfect RP voice, declared, "Oh, I rather adore a cream tea with Cornish clotted cream and a dab of caviar."

Sid blinked. "Blimey. Didn't know you had that in you."

"See? I can be classy when I want." Wendy lied. She could manage the odd sentence but no more than that.

They both looked up when the man who entered took a seat two tables away. Valentino, his wine-red suit faintly out of place among the beachgoers, sat with his tea untouched, watching. He'd caught only the last few words—the fine, lilting accent, the talk of cream tea and caviar. His eyes glowed like lamps behind glass.

When Sid left to chase another hopeless client, Valentino rose smoothly and approached.

"Forgive me for intruding," he said with a half-bow, his voice silken. "I couldn't help overhearing your performance. That accent it's exquisite. Natural elegance, rare in this part of the world."

Wendy blinked. "Oh, uh—thank you. I do bits of acting, yeah, I mean yes." She added returning to her posh tone

He smiled. "How delightful. I'm assembling a small but distinguished troupe for an exclusive theatrical enterprise. Intimate performances. Bespoke roles. You would be perfect."

Her eyes widened. "Really? Me?"

"But of course. You have that rare quality—presence, and class."

He leaned forward, lowering his voice confidentially. "I'm hosting an audition at my studio. Private, of course. Discretion is vital in this business."

It was flattery that did it—the words distinguished, bespoke, presence. After months of casting rejections, Wendy wanted to believe. She agreed to go with him, laughing off the warning bell in her head.

Valentino's workshop was tucked behind a shuttered amusement arcade. Wendy hesitated outside the peeling metal door, listening to the distant cry of seagulls and the clunking machinery of long-dead slot machines. This, she told herself, was still better than the commercial for discounted broadband she hadn't landed last week.

Valentino pushed the door open with theatrical flair.

Inside, the air was thick with sawdust and varnish, and rows of puppet heads stared from shelves: painted grins, blank eyes. Some had eyebrows too expressive, some not expressive enough. One had a moustache so large it seemed to judge her.

"Don't be intimidated," Valentino said, sweeping past them. "They're only jealous you still have a spinal column."

Wendy wasn't sure if he was joking.

The walls were lined with miniature scenery—tiny seaside sets, velvet curtains, the makings of worlds in miniature. Everything looked handcrafted, elaborate, and faintly menacing. Even the little beach huts seemed to be squinting at her.

"Well!" Valentino clapped his hands. "Let us begin your audition. I could tell you have presence. I sensed it when you asked for extra napkins at the café. Very authoritative."

Wendy cleared her throat. "Oh, well—thank you. I do try."

"Good. Confidence is vital. Now, let me see your movement."

"My movement?"

"Yes. Become a character. A creature. A force. Become… a small British breeze."

Wendy flapped her arms half-heartedly.

"No, no, that's a gust," Valentino corrected. "We need a breeze. Something that whispers secrets through the cracks of windows."

Wendy tried again, moving with the stiffness of someone who had once done a Zumba class and regretted it.

Valentino watched with rapturous concentration, nodding as though witnessing genius.

"Wonderful. Whispery. Unsettling. Yes." He circled her, hands clasped behind his back like an eccentric driving instructor.

"Next—emotional versatility. Give me fear."

Wendy widened her eyes.

"Bigger," Valentino said.

She widened them more until she looked like a startled goldfish.

"Excellent. Now—joy."

She attempted a smile. It came out strained, the expression of someone at a job interview being asked where they see themselves in five years. Valentino inhaled sharply. "Marvelous! Such tragic optimism!" He rummaged among his tools and handed her a wooden rod.

"Pretend this is your co-star."

Wendy held it. "Who am I talking to?"

"Anyone who has ever wronged you. Channel it."

She thought immediately of a casting director who told her she "had a very rest-based energy." She addressed the rod with professional fury. Valentino beamed. "Astonishing! You have rage wrapped in politeness. Audiences adore that."

She was beginning to suspect this was the strangest audition ever conducted, including the time she'd had to pretend to be a talking slice of cheese.

"Now, final skill test," Valentino said. "Show me stillness. Absolute, utter stillness. Think: deep existential dread, no refunds."
Wendy froze. Mostly because she didn't know what to do next. Valentino leaned in, whispering, "You are a natural marionette."

She hoped that was a compliment. He stepped back, hands pressed dramatically to his chest.

"My dear… you are everything I've been searching for. There is greatness in you. Hidden. Asleep. Slightly malnourished, perhaps, but present."

"Well," Wendy said, blushing despite her fear, "I do Pilates."

"Of course you do."

He gestured toward a small table draped with fabric that had once been velvet and now resembled melted liquorice.

"Just a little tea before we continue," he said, pouring from a chipped porcelain pot. "To calm the nerves."

Wendy accepted the cup. It trembled faintly in her hand as she raised it. The taste was sweet and oddly metallic. She frowned. "Is this—English Breakfast or Earl Grey? I know me teas you know." She gave Valentino a puzzled grin.

"Now," Valentino said, his tone suddenly hushed, reverent. "Every great transformation begins with surrender."

The workshop tilted. The puppet heads crept closer. The velvet curtains rippled like something breathing behind them. The room began to spin. The last thing Wendy saw was Valentino's face—blurry, magnified, smiling as though from a great distance.

Then, blackness.

The next sound was the clatter of an oversized door and Valentino's booming voice echoing through plastered walls.

"Ladies and gentlemen, your new leading lady—Miss Wendy Worthington!"

He was holding something between his palms, lowering it delicately into the doll's house living room like a stage prop. A figure, limp and curled, no taller than a loaf of bread.

Judy looked up from the miniature kitchen, fork in hand, whisking egg yolks as thick as cement. Brian and the background artists gathered together as Valentino set the new actress down and stepped back with pride.

Inside, Wendy stirred, groaned—and sat up.

Her eyes darted across the toy-sized furniture, the painted walls, the face staring down at her through the ceiling gap.

Then she screamed, a full-throated, furious sound:

"What the bleeding hell's goin' on? Where am I?!"

Brian jumped. "Blimey! We're not casting for EastEnders!"

Valentino's shadow loomed large outside the house. "Ah," he said, tone bright as champagne, "a method actress. So authentic."

Judy, calm as you please, leaned on the counter, the fork dangling from her hand. "Welcome to the company, darling," she said dryly. "You'll fit right in."

Wendy blinked up at her, trembling. "Company? What company? Who are you lot?"

"The Punch and Judy Repertory Ensemble," Brian said proudly, puffing out his chest. "Managed by yours truly."

Judy rolled her eyes. "Managed, he says. I'd call it tolerated."

Valentino's fingers drummed on the doll's house roof. "Now, now, let's not bicker on a lady's first day. Miss Worthington is going to bring refinement to our repertoire."

"She's got refinement, all right," Judy muttered. "About as much as a bacon sandwich."

Valentino ignored her, beaming at Wendy. "Rest now, my dear. Tomorrow, rehearsal begins. We open with A Midsummer Night's Dream. I see you as Titania."

"I ain't playin' no bleedin' fairy!" Wendy shouted, voice cracking.

Valentino's grin widened. "Oh, you'll play it beautifully. I can tell. You have magic in you."

He closed the doll's house roof gently, and the sound of the latch was as final as a coffin lid.

That night, as the stage lights dimmed above and as the sound of the sea seemed to press faintly against the walls, Brian stood by the doll's house window, looking out at the workshop beyond—the rows of heads, the painted scenery, the half-finished faces waiting to be given life.

He whispered, almost admiringly, "He's got plans, our Valentino. Big ones."

Judy stirred the pot on the tiny stove, the smell of garlic rising warm and sharp. "Yeah," she said. "And every plan of his starts with someone else getting smaller."

Wendy sat at the miniature table, head in her hands, sobbing quietly.

"Don't cry, love," Brian said gently. "You'll get used to it."

She looked up, eyes wide, furious.
"Used to it? You're all mad! I want me life back!"

Her voice echoed through the doll's-house kitchen, far too large a sound for such a tiny body. The others fell quiet. Even Brian's relentless cheer dimmed.
Judy stepped toward her, a tissue cut from a napkin in her hand. Up close, Wendy could see the exhaustion in her face — the kind that came from months of fear, not a lack of sleep. Judy's hands trembled slightly as she passed the tissue over, as though the truth of their situation still shook her too.

"We all do, darling. But the show goes on."

She tried to smile, but it faltered. Her eyes darted to the lace-curtained window, checking — always checking — for Valentino's shadow.

"Listen to me," Judy said, her voice tightening with a quiet desperation. "We're not puppets. We're not props. We're people. He shrank us. Stole us. And once you're this size, once he puts you in the house… you don't get to leave. You don't get to go back. You're trapped in a world where even the sugar bowl can kill you if you trip into it." She swallowed hard.

"It's like being kidnapped, only worse — because no one out there knows you're missing. They'll think you just left, or gave up, or moved on. They'll never imagine you're in here, living in some madman's dollhouse."

Wendy stared at her, stunned.

Judy's voice dropped to a trembling whisper.

"We can't go back to who we were. We've tried. All of us. And failing at that… that's the worst part. Remembering the world you came from but not being able to reach it."

Outside, Valentino's shadow moved across the workshop wall, slow and deliberate, like a curtain falling.

Chapter 5

The Seaside Spotlight

Torquay, Friday Night.

The theatre was a cracked jewel — chipped paint, threadbare velvet curtains, a chandelier that rattled whenever the bass kicked too hard. But the energy inside?

Electric.

The crowd was mixed and mismatched — young lads hiding behind cheap lager pints, older gentlemen with nervous smiles and memories of hiding who they were for decades.

This wasn't Soho. This was Devon, and the walls of the "Harlequin Palace" held secrets tighter than most brothels. Raymondo burst onto the stage in a cascade of sequins and sweat — a storm wrapped in purple satin. He wasn't built like the others. He wasn't lean or lithe. He wasn't "drag-race material," as cruel judges might say. No — Ray was big. Big in presence, big in curves, big in heart.

A big, beautiful nightclub goddess in heels that defied physics. He moved with a grace that shouldn't have belonged to him — every gesture precise, every turn a study in balance. His face caught the spotlight like it had been carved for it. Perfect cheekbones. Wild eyes. Smile like a razor. Sweat poured down his temples. Mascara threatened to run. He didn't care. Tonight, he was alive.

Ray sang — or rather, lip-synced — but there was something hypnotic in it. His mouth formed every word like it was gospel. His body swept across the stage in arcs of silk and fierce determination. He caught eyes deliberately — held them — owned them. The nervous boy in row three, clutching his coat like armour?

Ray winked — and the boy's blush lit up the room. The older gent in the back who still wore his wedding ring? Ray blew him a kiss — and the man laughed for the first time in months. Raymondo was church for the lost. A revelation for the lonely. A home for those who had none.

The finale hit — glitter falling from the beams, the backing track crashing into its last triumphant note. Ray struck his pose — leg extended, hand on hip, eyes blazing.

Then silence.

Then cheers — louder than the theatre deserved, long enough to drown the second-hand sadness of the entire place. He bowed — small, humble, but burning with pride. Curtains closed and the lights dimmed.

Ray leaned against the stage wall, panting, peeling off his wig slightly to let his scalp breathe. His chest heaved; sweat dripped from his brow. He wasn't ashamed of it — passion cost energy, darling. A familiar voice drifted toward him, dry as stale sherry.

"You look like you've been marinating in your own juices, Ray."

Derrick — assistant stage manager — short, sallow, and cynical. A clipboard always welded to his hand like it had grown there. Ray fanned himself dramatically. "Derrick, sweetheart, that's not sweat — that's glamour leaking out."

Derrick snorted. "If glamour smelled like curry and cheap vodka, you'd win every award."

Ray clicked his tongue. "Don't be jealous. Some of us were born with pizzazz."

"You were born with cholesterol," Derrick muttered.

Ray smacked him lightly on the arm with a feather boa. "Low blow. Besides, I make it work. Plenty of queens bigger than me."

"One or two," Derrick said. "And they weren't in Torquay next to broken chairs and sticky carpets."

Ray tilted his chin up, eyes glittering. "That's why I want my own slot, darling. Proper billing. Poster in the foyer. Maybe even one of those neon signs with my name on it — Raymondo the Magnificent."

Derrick stared at him. "Ray... this place barely survives on bingo nights."

"So we change that," Ray said, face suddenly serious.

"People come here because I make them feel something. I bring joy. I bring life." He leaned closer. "I deserve a spot. A serious one."

Derrick sighed, defeated but fond.

"I'll talk to Graham. He hates good ideas, but I'll talk to him."

Ray glowed. "You little darling! I knew you liked me."

"I don't," Derrick muttered. "I'm terrified of you."

Ray laughed — loud, shameless, infectious.

As Derrick left, Ray stood for a moment alone, breathing slowly, staring out through the slight gap in the curtains where he could still see the last of the crowd drifting into the night. He whispered to himself — soft, hopeful, almost prayerful: "One day, Raymondo… you'll be centre stage. Centre of everything."

And the stage lights — barely working, flickered and hummed as if they heard him.

He didn't know what waited for him.

Not yet.

But fate had already begun to turn.

Chapter 6

Rehearsal for a Dream

The miniature theatre glowed like a jewel box under its ceiling of dust-flecked light. Red velvet curtains framed the stage; gold balconies curled delicately along the sides like sugared icing. Even the air seemed thinner here, perfumed faintly with polish and the ghost of burnt glue. Somewhere above, the sea shushed faintly against the promenade, and the mechanical hum of the fairground seeped down through the rafters like a lullaby gone wrong.

Valentino sat in his director's chair—carved, gilded, entirely too large for the scale of the room. He leaned forward, elbows on knees, eyes gleaming with manic purpose.

"Places, everyone! Brian, you're Oberon—commanding, jealous, cruel but charming. Wendy, you are Titania—the essence of grace. A queen of moonlight, not of margarine adverts."

Wendy adjusted her crown, which looked suspiciously like a bottle cap spray-painted silver. "Yeah, all right," she muttered. "Got it."

"From Act Two, Scene One," Valentino announced, sweeping a hand like a maestro before an invisible orchestra. "And... begin!"
The tiny stage lights flared on. Brian stepped forward first, chest puffed, voice trembling with earnest grandeur.

"How now, spirit! Whither wander you?"

The line came out halfway between Olivier and a foghorn, but he believed every syllable. Judy, perched on the balcony, flicked through a tiny copy of Miniature Home Living, Valentino had shrunk for her and sighed audibly.

Then came Wendy's turn. She rose from her flowery bed—made from scraps of old silk and glitter—and delivered her opening line with full, unselfconscious force.

"What angel wakes me from me bloomin' flowery bed?"

The sound bounced off the gilt walls like a pub argument.

Valentino flinched as though struck. "Bloomin'? BLOOMIN'? No, no, no, my darling! 'From my flowery bed.' Enunciate. Round the vowels like pearls."

"That's what I did do," Wendy shot back. "Flowery bed. You just don't like my accent."

He plastered on a smile. "Art transcends accent."

"Well, art's just gonna have to cope," she said, folding her arms. "This is how I talk."

Brian, ever the diplomat, jumped in: "It's got character, Val. Real working-class energy! Titania from Tilbury—it's fresh!"

"Titania from Tilbury," Judy repeated without looking up. "Has a nice ring. You could put it on a tea towel."

The background artists snorted, trying not to laugh. Valentino's head swivelled toward them like an owl's.

"Silence!" he barked. "We are not at Butlins. We are conjuring artistry!"

The laughter died. Wendy rolled her eyes but went again.

"What angel wakes me from me bloomin'—sorry—flowery bed?"

Valentino twitched visibly. His hands fluttered in midair like nervous birds. "Again! This time, with dreaminess! Think moonlight. Think gossamer. Think Glyndebourne, not Green Street Market!"

Wendy frowned. "Who's Glyndebourne when she's at home?"

Brian stage-whispered, "Opera house."

"Opera? Oh, la-di-da." Wendy straightened her crown again, giving it a little tilt. "Right. From me—flowery—bed." She pronounced every syllable as if chewing toffee.

"What angel wakes me from me bloomin'—sorry—flowery—bloomin' bed?"

Judy put down her magazine and clapped slowly. "Shakespeare's spinning in his grave like a wind turbine."

Valentino's face froze in a smile so tight it could have cracked porcelain. "Let us take it again," he said, voice like glass. "From the top."

Brian launched in with renewed vigour, declaiming like a man possessed. He forgot his second line and improvised grandly, quoting from the wrong scene entirely. His foot caught one of the fairy extras, who yelped and toppled over, strings tangling.

"Oh! Sorry, love!" Brian said, scooping the limp fairy up and propping her on a toadstool. "Got a bit carried away. Happens in the moment."

Judy muttered, "You trample your co-stars in the moment."

"Art demands sacrifice," Brian replied, straight-faced.

Valentino stood, clapping his hands once. "Again! Energy! Urgency! Elegance!"

Wendy sighed and delivered the line for what felt like the fifteenth time. Each attempt sounded broader, brasher, more defiantly herself.

"What angel wakes me from me bloomin' flowery bed, then? You better not've trod on me pansies!"

The background artists collapsed into helpless giggles. Judy was practically wheezing.

Valentino's shadow stretched long and thin across the stage, fingers twitching as though he might pluck her from it. "Enough!" he roared. "Enough of this… this mockery!"

He strode onto the stage, boots thudding like thunder, knocking a scenery panel slightly askew. "Do you think Shakespeare wrote for the amusement of dockworkers? No! He wrote for royalty!"

"Well, I ain't royalty," Wendy shot back. "And neither are you, luv. You're a fella in a red suit talking to toys."

The silence that followed was sharp enough to cut glass.

Valentino smiled—slowly, dangerously. "That," he said softly, "was unwise."

He drew himself up to his full, impossible height, towering over the stage. His shadow loomed across the backdrop like a monstrous marionette.

"You will speak with grace," he said, his voice low but thrumming with anger. "You will become art. Do you understand?"

Wendy glared up at him, her hands trembling—but not from fear. Something behind her eyes flickered, anger perhaps or something stranger. When she spoke, her voice had a quiet steel.

"I'll speak how I like, luv."

It wasn't loud, but it carried, echoing faintly through the doll's house theatre.

For the first time, Valentino's expression faltered. His hand shook on the control bar above the stage. The lights flickered; one of the spotlight bulbs gave a small, electric pop. The strings trembled, though he hadn't moved them.

Brian looked up nervously. "Bit of static, maybe?"

Valentino didn't answer. He just stared at Wendy—small, defiant, very much alive in a way that didn't seem to belong in his world.

"Again," he growled finally. "From the top."

"Make up your mind," Judy muttered, crossing her legs. "You'll have her doing this till she's speaking in tongues."

Wendy smirked. "Fairies, magic, dreams—who's to say I ain't?"

They began once more. Brian, shaken but game, bellowed his opening. Wendy followed, this time softer—mockingly delicate.

"What angel wakes me from me flowery bed?"

Valentino nodded approvingly—then flinched as her next words came through rough as sandpaper.

"'Oo's makin' all that racket? Some people tryin' to kip!"

The background artists broke into laughter again. Judy snorted tea through her nose.

Valentino slammed his script shut. "ENOUGH! You're ruining it!"

"She's improvin' it," Judy countered, deadpan. "First time anyone's believed a word of this."

"Silence!" he roared.

A heavy stillness fell — the kind that didn't belong in a comedy, Shakespearean or otherwise. The tiny actors froze mid-gesture, terrified of breathing wrong. Above them, towering and twitching with irritation, Valentino loomed like an impatient god whose creations had learnt the meaning of chaos.

He stepped closer to the miniature stage, his shadow swallowing them.

"I give you art," he hissed, "and you give me… this."

Brian whimpered. Judy folded her arms. Wendy raised an eyebrow, already unimpressed by tyranny, whether full-sized or otherwise.

Valentino's eye twitched. "Again," he ordered. "And this time—no accents, no improvisation, no… personality."

His fingers brushed the strings overhead — the threat unmistakable.

Wendy swallowed. Judy muttered something unsavoury. Brian adjusted his cap with the solemn air of a man preparing for execution.

They shuffled back into position.

Above them, Valentino inhaled sharply, bracing himself.

Below him, the shrunken cast exhaled collectively — the resigned, exhausted sigh of people who knew the show must go on, mostly because the alternative was worse.

The rehearsal restarted. But now, every one of them knew: This wasn't Shakespeare anymore.
This was survival.

The rehearsal restarted.

They moved stiffly, each step measured, each breath held as if the very air might snap under tension. A strange vibration began above them—soft at first, like distant machinery warming up. Brian glanced upward. Judy muttered, "Oh, that's never good." Even Wendy, defiant as she was, felt the hairs on her neck rise.

The hum deepened. A faint tremor travelled through the miniature floorboards. Something in the theatre was waking up. Or breaking down. The stage lights flickered violently. Dust rained from the rafters. One of the fairy extras shrieked as her strings began to smoke—thin, white wisps curling upward like incense. The smell was sharp, electric, almost metallic.

Then—snap.

The little puppet crumpled mid-line, collapsing onto the painted grass, its tiny crown rolling away.

Everyone froze.

Brian's mouth hung open. "Blimey. She's gone all limp."

Valentino stooped, plucking the fairy up between thumb and forefinger. The strings were scorched to black threads, fused into her back like veins turned to wire. "A… technical fault," he muttered. "Nothing more."

Judy's eyes narrowed. "That's what you said last time."

Valentino shot her a warning glare. "There was no last time."

She leaned toward Wendy, voice low. "It's starting again."

Wendy blinked. "What is?"

Judy's face gave nothing away. "You'll see."

Valentino cleared his throat, forcing his voice into brightness. "We'll stop here for today. Tomorrow, we perfect Act Three. Rest your voices—and your attitudes."

He turned, cloak sweeping dramatically as he exited through the side curtain, his laughter echoing behind him—thin, artificial, and just slightly cracked.

They sat in silence after he'd gone. The only sound was the faint hum of the fans that kept air drifting through the doll's house. The smell of burnt string lingered like something once alive.

Brian crouched beside the collapsed fairy puppet, examining the scorched filaments. "Strange," he murmured. "It's like they burned themselves."

"Everything burns eventually," Judy said. She stood, stretching, her shadow moving across the painted floor. "Even divas."

Wendy was still sitting on the edge of the stage, legs dangling, her reflection glinting in a bit of broken mirror. "What's wrong with him?" she asked softly. "He's mental, that one. Proper gone."

Judy gave a dry smile that didn't reach her eyes. "You're not the first to notice."

"Then why don't you rebel, stop doing what he wants?" Wendy asked, voice almost pleading.

Judy turned her head, and for a heartbeat her face looked older—hollow, almost translucent in the dim light.

"Because we can't, you don't know what he can do to us Wendy. All of us."

The words seemed to echo, faint but real, even after she stopped speaking. A ripple passed through the strings above them—so gentle it might have been a draft, except that every puppet in the dressing room twitched once, as if in answer.

Brian looked up, nervous, pretending not to see. "Don't be so grim, Jude. It's the theatre. Tempers flare, egos clash, strings snap. It's part of the magic."

"Magic," Judy repeated flatly. "That what you call it?"

He grinned, undeterred. "Course. We're part of something bigger, aren't we? Art in miniature! Shakespeare reborn! Valentino's got a vision."

Wendy snorted. "Yeah, well, his vision nearly singed my fringe."

Judy smiled thinly. "Consider yourself lucky. Last actress didn't even get a line out before—"

She stopped. Something flickered across her face, a shadow of memory. "—well, never mind."

Wendy turned sharply. "Before what?"

But Judy was already walking away, humming under her breath. Brian followed, tidying the props. One by one, the little stage lights blinked out until only the faint glow of the control booth remained, silhouetting the tall, still figure of Valentino watching from above.

Wendy looked up. The shadow didn't move, but she could feel it staring back.

For a moment, she could swear she heard whispering—the faintest chorus of voices, fluttering like moths in the rafters. She couldn't tell if they were laughing, crying, or calling her name.

Then the lights cut completely, leaving her in darkness.

When dawn crept through the cracks of the workshop shutters, the dolls' house sat silent, perfect, and still. But deep inside, at the centre of the tiny stage, Titania's crown glimmered faintly—as if catching light from somewhere unseen.

Not the light of morning, nor candle, nor lantern.

A secret light.

A remembering light.

It pulsed—once, like a heartbeat. Dust motes spiralled around it, pulled as though by breath from a mouth that had no lungs. The velvet curtains at the miniature stage stirred, though no draft passed through the workshop. The painted backdrop shimmered, colours deepening, shadows lengthening, as if the house slept and dreamed, and the dreams were slipping out through the cracks.

And then came the smallest sound—too small for a human ear, too sharp for silence to ignore.

A metallic tap.

A trembling shift in the crown's setting, the tiniest echo of movement. As though some invisible hand had tried it on, just for a moment—

And found that it fit

Chapter 7

Ray

Backstage Send-Off

Ray sat at the long mirror in the cramped dressing room, wiping eyeliner smudges from beneath his eyes. Sequins clung to the carpet like confetti from a party long gone, and someone's abandoned wig sat on a hatstand, glaring at everyone with cruelly arched eyebrows.

Behind him, the room buzzed. Laughter, perfume, chatter — the sort of pre-performance chaos that only drag artists could manage while still looking fabulous.

At the centre of it stood Stevie Starlight — smaller than Ray, thin as ribbon, platinum wig cascading to his shoulders, glitter eyeshadow thick enough to choke a horse. Stevie was radiant tonight, pacing the room like some overexcited poodle in heels.

"London, babes!" He cried, throwing up jazz hands. "Well — Barking. But Barking is PRETTY MUCH London if you squint and ignore the fact the building ga are a bit shorter."

Ray clutched his heart dramatically.

"London! You're leaving me for London? Betrayal, darling. Absolute betrayal." Stevie shrieked with laughter. "You told me to audition, you daft cow!"

"I know, but I didn't mean you'd actually get it!" Ray sniffed loudly. "I wanted you to fail so I could look noble comforting you."

Stevie flung an arm around Ray. "You're my fairy godmother."

Ray corrected him. "Fairy dragmother."

A cheer went up from the room. Someone uncorked cheap prosecco. Glitter flew everywhere. Wigs bounced. They were queens and misfits and miracles — and tonight, they were sending their sister off to his big(ish) break.

Stevie raised his glass. "To Raymondo the Magnificent — who gave me the number for that audition and never once tried to sabotage me."

Ray blinked innocently. "I absolutely considered it but then I remembered I'm a humanitarian."

A roar of laughter.

Someone pushed a slice of supermarket cake into Stevie's face. Stevie screeched dramatically. Ray held him lovingly while he cleaned it off. Then, quieter, the tone shifted. "You could have auditioned, Ray," Stevie said. "You would've been incredible."

Ray shrugged, adjusting his sequined bodice. "My mum needs me here. Dad's gone, the family's big. Someone's gotta help her keep them all fed."

Stevie nodded, eyes soft. "She's lucky to have you."

Ray waved a hand dismissively. "I'll get my chance one day. The world can wait a minute." But his reflection in the mirror — beneath the rouge and the lashes — held something fragile. Dreams cost; he'd pay later. Tonight was Stevie's night.

They partied. They danced. They joked. They hugged with mascara-muddy tears. And in the middle of it all — Ray felt fiercely happy for Stevie. The sort of happiness that didn't come with envy, just… love.

The morning rush at "Café Latte Haven" was chaotic. A queue practically pushed through the door and Ray — apron on, hair tied back, singing under his breath — worked the coffee machine like a magician at a circus.

"Flat white, extra hot, no foam!" He sang, sliding a cup down the counter like a bowling ball.

"Raymondo, you're a menace," the old man laughed.

"Thank you, darling — I aim to please."

Ray could sing. Not pretend singing. Proper singing. Warm, strong, roughed at the edges — like whisky and honey. He hummed a gospel riff and the whole café paused to listen. Then the bell over the door jingled.

"Mama!" Ray called.

His mother swept in; her Caribbean-print headscarf bright as hibiscus flowers. Round-cheeked, regal, loving. She handed him a Tupperware box. "I made plantain fritters for your lunch, baby."

Ray kissed her cheek noisily. "You're a goddess in human form."

"You eating proper?" She asked, stern but soft, eyeing him up and down with theatrical suspicion.

"When am I not?" Ray smirked, patting his stomach like a drum.

She clicked her tongue. "Hmph. You better be. Your mama worked too hard to raise a fine boy just for him to fade away."

He rolled his eyes. "Fade away? Look at the size of me, Ma. You think I got this big in breadcrumbs alone?"

She narrowed her eyes with mock severity. "I like you having a bit of weight. Shows you're cared for. Shows your mama feeds you right."

Ray laughed, scooping her into a gentle hug. "Trust me, Ma, nobody's confusing me for a salad."

She flicked a napkin at him. "Don't you sass me. I raised you better than sass."

He winked. "You raised me on sass."

She grinned despite herself. "True."

The customers adored this ritual. Ray adored her. "Mama, listen — I'm heading straight to the theatre after work. So I won't need dinner tonight."

She clasped his hands. "i'll save you some. For tomorrow."

She looked at him a moment longer — seeing something under his cheeky grin. "You'll make it one day," she said quietly. He didn't answer. He kissed her forehead instead.

Latr that night at The Harlequin Palace Ray was a storm. A glitter hurricane. But tonight, he didn't lip-sync — he sang. And every note throbbed with emotion.

The trouble was the pianist. Bless him — small, terrified man with the musical ear of a seasick goat. He hit bum notes like they offended him personally. The audience laughed kindly, thinking it was all part of the comedy. Ray did not laugh. Between verses, under his breath: "I will shove this piano up his backside if he hits that key again."

After the final bow, he stormed backstage, Derrick scrambling after him. "It's not my fault!" Derrick squeaked. "We can't afford better!"

Ray paced like a panther. "Tape would be better!"

"It skips."

"So does he!"

Derrick gave up. "Just… just read your bloody note."

Ray froze. "What note?"

Derrick handed over a folded card. Ray opened it cautiously. The handwriting was neat. Elegant. Precise:

> **"My compliments on your performance. You have presence, power, and potential.**
> *Meet with me — tomorrow — to discuss a leading role in my troupe Valentino"*

Ray reread it. Once. Twice. Three times. The he fell into the chair. "Valentino?" he whispered.

Derrick raised an eyebrow. "Who's Valentino?"

Ray stared ahead, voice soft, awed.

"Someone who might just change everything."

Chapter 8

Small Revolutions

Morning came late in the workshop. The sunlight slanted in through high windows clouded with dust, pooling faintly over the puppet theatre stage. The air still smelled of last night's burnt string — sharp, metallic, like a whisper of something alive that refused to die.

Inside the dolls' house, Wendy was the first to stir. She sat at the tiny kitchen table in a robe stitched from what looked like a silk handkerchief, her crown pushed askew on the counter beside a cup no larger than a thimble. Judy was already there, cutting stale crumbs of bread into smaller crumbs, the knife moving with unhurried precision.

"Sleep all right?" Judy asked without looking up.

"Did I bollocks," Wendy muttered. "Kept hearing whispering. Thought it was the pipes."

"It's never the pipes," Judy said quietly.

Wendy glanced toward the theatre ceiling, where the faint outlines of strings still hung like spiderwebs in the shadows. "You mean… them?"

Judy didn't answer. She wiped her hands and sat opposite her. "How are your nerves, love?"

"My nerves are fine. My patience is another story." Wendy leaned back, folding her arms. "I ain't built for this, Jude. I'm an actress, not a flipping ornament. He can't keep us like this."

Judy gave a short, humourless laugh. "He can. He has. For years."

That silenced them both. Somewhere outside, the faint mechanical tune of a carousel leaked through the window — cheerful, oblivious.

After a moment, Wendy said, "There's got to be a way. If he can make us small, he can make us big again."

Judy's face darkened. "That's what the last one said."

"The last what?"

Judy busied herself with the bread again. "Doesn't matter. She didn't last long enough to find out."

Wendy frowned. "And Brian?"

"Oh, Brian's happy as Larry. Thinks he's starring at the Old Vic. Doesn't see the strings at all."

There was a pause, and then Wendy grinned crookedly. "Well, maybe it's time someone cut a few."

By the time Valentino arrived for rehearsal, the troupe was already assembled. He swept into the workshop in his crimson coat, his presence filling the room like a stage direction: Enter Showman, grand and gleaming.

"Ah, my darlings!" he cried, throwing his arms wide. "Did we dream of greatness? Did the muse visit us in the night?"

Brian straightened immediately. "Ready and eager, Val! Been practising my verse since dawn."

"Splendid! A true professional."

Judy yawned. "Some of us were trying to sleep."

Valentino ignored her. His gaze moved to Wendy. "And you, my Titania? Ready to reign in moonlit splendour once more?"

Wendy smiled sweetly. "Born ready, luv."

Something in her tone made him blink — a subtle confidence, like a note slightly off-key. "Excellent. From Act Three, the lovers' quarrel. Let us see your fury, your passion, your… transcendence."

The lights snapped on. Brian took his mark opposite her, chest puffed.

"Why should Titania cross her Oberon?" he declaimed, voice ringing off the tiny rafters.

Wendy's reply came fast, hard, and entirely unrefined:
"'Cause you nicked the kid, that's why! Give 'im back or I'll box your ears, you daft fairy!"

Judy coughed to hide a laugh. The background artists snorted openly.

Valentino's smile faltered. "No, no, no! Not 'daft fairy.' Try 'jealous lord.' You are ethereal, majestic!"

"I'm bloody furious, that's what I am," Wendy shot back. "You want majestic, write it in the script!"

His eyes flashed. "I am the script."

The words hung in the air like thunder. For a moment, even the strings above seemed to tense.

Wendy met his gaze, unflinching. "Then maybe it's time someone rewrote it."

The rehearsal disintegrated from there.

Brian, ever the optimist, tried to keep the scene alive, delivering speeches no one else had rehearsed and ending each with a flourish. The background artists moved sluggishly, their faces pale, their strings occasionally twitching of their own accord.

Judy stayed back, watching — her eyes on Valentino rather than the stage. She noticed how his control bar trembled slightly, how sweat glistened at his temples. The perfectionist was fraying.

When Wendy refused to soften her accent, he demanded another take. When she rolled her eyes, he shouted for silence. The lights flickered again. A faint, electric hum threaded the air, like static building.

At one point, Wendy raised a hand to gesture, and every string in the room seemed to sway gently with her. It might have been coincidence — or something else.

Valentino froze mid-instruction. "Who moved that?"

No one answered.

He scanned the ceiling, suspicion narrowing his eyes. Then, softly, he said, "Very well. We shall take a short break."

Back in the dressing room, Wendy was grinning. "Did you see his face? He thought the ceiling was haunted."

"Maybe it is," Judy said.

"Or maybe," Wendy replied, lowering her voice, "he's not the only one who can pull strings."

Judy stared at her. "What are you saying?"

"I'm saying I felt something. When he got angry, I got angrier — and something… shifted. Like the air listened."

Judy gave a wary frown. "Careful, love. That's how it starts."

"How what starts?"

"The change. The others — they said the same. Thought they could fight him. Thought they could turn it back on him."

"What happened?"

"They burned."

The word landed heavy.

But Wendy only smiled, a slow, stubborn curve of the mouth. "Then I'll burn brighter."

That evening, after Valentino locked the workshop and left, the dolls' house came alive with murmurs. Brian rehearsed lines under his breath, pacing the sitting room. The background artists whispered in corners.

And in the kitchen, under the faint glow of a match-sized lamp, Judy and Wendy sat over cups of cold tea.

Wendy leaned close. "You said we can't be free. But that ain't true, is it? He's got control — but it's not perfect. You saw what happened today."

"I saw you nearly set the ceiling alight," Judy said.

"Then it's working."

Judy rubbed her temples. "You don't understand. We're not actors anymore. We're part of him — his imagination, his strings, his bloody vanity."

"Then maybe we start pulling him apart from the inside."

For a long moment, Judy said nothing. Her face was unreadable. Then, finally: "If you're going to pick a fight with Valentino, you'll need allies."

"Brian?"

Judy snorted. "Brian would side with a lamppost if it applauded him."

"Then the background mob? But they're frightened Wendy."

"But frightened people can be useful" Wendy grinned.

Chapter 9

New Additions.

Ray Ramondo had never been late for an audition in his life. Not once. Not when he sang in a half-flooded nightclub in Croydon, nor when he was chased out of a Soho cabaret for "redecorating" the stage curtains with glitter glue. Stardom, he told himself, was a matter of showing up—fully padded, fully painted, and fully ready.

He hummed softly as he dressed, his solid frame brushing the dressing table and wardrobe with each unhurried movement. Piece by piece he collected his attire, pausing only to tuck a curtain of dark hair behind one ear. His palms swept appreciatively across his torso, and a slow smile of satisfaction crept onto his face.

Bust pads? He opened the drawer and surveyed his options like a general choosing weapons. Forty-two double D, for polite company. Forty-two double F, for the impact. He went with the latter. "If they can't handle an entrance," he told his reflection, "They don't deserve the show."

Fishnets, check.

Purple satin gown, snug but forgiving, check.

Heels high enough to cause altitude sickness, check.

He puckered up, dabbed on a final smear of lipstick—shade: "Cabaret Cranberry"—and winked. "Showtime, darling."

He strutted down the hallway of his tiny flat, each step an overture. Outside, the morning glittered. The pavements weren't paved with gold, not quite—but they gleamed like sequins under the London sun, and that was close enough for Ray. Today, at last, someone would see him for the star he truly was.

Valentino's workshop looked exactly like the kind of place that made stars—or broke them.

When Ray knocked, the door swung open to reveal a tall man in a waistcoat and immaculate cravat, eyes dark as marionette joints. "Mr Ramondo," Valentino purred, smoothing his tie. "So glad you could attend."

"Pleasure's mine, honey," said Ray, sweeping in like a carnival in human form. "Now where do you want me—stage left, centre spotlight, or draped over the piano?"

Valentino chuckled. "Let's begin with tea, perhaps."

"Oh, how frightfully civilised! Usually, I start auditions by being told I'm 'too much.'" He fluttered a hand. "Imagine that. Too much."

Valentino smiled in that unfathomable way of his, the kind that didn't quite reach his eyes. "On the contrary. I suspect you'll be just enough."

"Then sugar and scandal it is," said Ray, taking the offered cup with a flourish. "Would you like me to start with a song? I do a marvellous 'I Could Have Danced All Night.' Got me a standing ovation once—well, half-standing, they were mostly drunk."

"By all means," said Valentino, eyes glinting. "Let's see… your interpretation."

Ray straightened, poised, and the air seemed to hush. He began to sing—softly at first, a smoky purr, then rising into a bright, aching sweetness that filled the room like perfume. The notes wobbled only slightly on the high end, but his face glowed with life.

"I could have danced all night, and still have begged for more…"

When he finished, Valentino was smiling—truly smiling this time.

"My dear," he said, "you are… magnificent."

Ray preened. "Oh, stop. You'll ruin my mascara."

"On the contrary," Valentino said softly, "I think I've only just begun."

When Brian came yawning down the stairs the next morning, it took him all of three seconds to realise something was different. For one, the faint scent of perfume and talcum powder hung in the air. For another, someone was snoring loudly on the miniature sofa, sprawled like a toppled goddess.

"Bloody hell!" Brian blurted.

The figure stirred. A tangle of purple fabric shifted, and a muffled voice said, "If that's room service, darling, tell them I ordered champagne, not shock."

"Who the devil are you?"

"Ray Ramondo, sweetheart," came the reply. "Star of stage, screen, and small disasters."

Brian blinked. "Do you know where you are?"

Ray opened one perfectly made-up eye and looked around the tiny room. The doll-sized furniture. The unfamiliar ceiling with its tangle of strings.

He sat up fast. "Oh, hell no!"

At that moment, the workshop roof creaked. Valentino's enormous face appeared through the window, smiling with delighted pride. "Isn't it wonderful!" he boomed. "I'm expanding the company!"

On seeing the giant appear through the roof Ray shrieked and passed out on the sofa.

"Expanding?" Brain repeated faintly.

"We'll be a family," Valentino said. "A complete company. You'll all thank me later."

He closed the roof again. The light dimmed.

Ray stirred and clutched his gown. "Tell me that was a fever dream."

"Nope," said Judy, emerging with a cup of thimble tea. "Welcome to the show."

It took Ray several hours—and a few theatrical breakdowns—to grasp the situation.

"So you're telling me, "He said, pacing, "that we're puppets."

"Miniaturised actors," corrected Brian. "He prefers that term."

"Well, I prefer alive and full-sized, but apparently nobody cares what I think." Ray fanned himself dramatically. "I've played tight stages before, but this is ridiculous."

"Sit down before you tear your seams," Judy advised. "You'll get used to it."

Ray glared. "Do I look like someone who gets used to anything? I reinvent, darling. Adaptations for background dancers."

"Then reinvent your expectations," Wendy said from the doorway. "He's not letting us out."

Ray turned. "And who might you be, Queen of the Fairies?"

"Wendy," she said flatly. "And yes, I am."

Ray tilted his head, then smiled. "Fabulous. Every troupe needs one woman who looks like she could win a fight."

Wendy smirked. "Careful, luv. I usually do."

That earned a laugh from Judy. Even Brian cracked a grin.

For the first time in years, perhaps, someone extraordinary had entered their strange little world—and the air felt different. Brighter. Louder. A touch more dangerous.

The next morning came with chaos.

A shrill cry sliced through the dollhouse like a siren. "I want my mummy! Mummy!"

Everyone bolted upright.

"Was that—?" Judy began.

"A child," Wendy said grimly.

They raced into the sitting room. There, perched on the tiny sofa with his face streaked in tears, was a little boy—no more than eight years old, in a ragged costume coat two sizes too big.

Valentino's shadow fell across them as he opened the roof again, beaming. "Meet Jack," he announced. "He's going to play Oliver Twist in my new production!"

The boy wailed, terrified.

Ray stepped forward before anyone else could move. He knelt—and softened his voice. "Hey there, poppet. Don't cry. You're all right."

Jack looked up, sniffling. "Where's my mum?"

"She's… probably wondering where you've got to," Ray said gently. "But you're safe for now, all right? Promise."

Behind him, Wendy's face was thunder. "Poor little mite. He's gone too far this time."

Valentino didn't seem to hear her. "Rehearsals will begin this afternoon. Such potential! Such innocence! The audience will weep!"

Then he shut the roof again.

Jack burst into tears.

Ray gathered him close. "Oh, sweetheart. You shouldn't be here."

Wendy's jaw clenched. "None of us should."

They met that evening in the kitchen. The lamp flickered over their faces—Wendy fierce, Judy thoughtful, Brian anxious, Ray radiant even in fatigue.

"We can't keep pretending," Wendy said. "He's not just playing director anymore. He's collecting us."

"Like action figures," Judy murmured. "With feelings."

Ray smoothed Jack's hair, the child now fast asleep beside him. "His parents must be going crazy. Poor little lad must be bewildered."

"Ray," Wendy said quietly, "you saw how scared he was. You must've felt it."

Ray's voice cracked. Just slightly. "Course I did." He took a steadying breath, straightened his shoulders. "Which is exactly why we're not staying like this."

Brian frowned. "And how do you propose we change that? He's got the controls."

Ray gave a small, dangerous smile. "Then we learn to pull a few of our own."

Judy raised an eyebrow. "You don't mean—?"

"Oh, darling, I absolutely do," Ray said, his voice a blend of silk and steel. "I've made men fall for me, clubs burn for me and I once convinced a bouncer I was Liza Minnelli's cousin. If there's a way out of this, I'll find it—and I'll do it in heels."

Wendy grinned. "Now that's the spirit."

For a moment, even in their fragile, painted forms, they felt like actors again—alive, plotting, dangerous.

Above them, unseen, a single string trembled. Then another.

Something in the workshop's dark corners stirred, as if listening.

That night, long after the lights went out, Ray couldn't sleep. Jack murmured in his slumber. Wendy shifted restlessly, caught between waking and sleep. The dolls' house creaked like a ship on dark water.

Ray stared up at the ceiling, whispering to the shadows. His mind churned—planning, plotting, dissecting every moment with Valentino, hunting for cracks in the man's armour. Had he missed something? Was there a flaw, a fracture, a way to break him? There had to be. Somewhere, buried in the madness of their miniature existence, was the key to ending it. And Ray was determined to find it.

"You want a show, Valentino?" he murmured. "You've got one."

He reached for the air—and for a heartbeat, the strings above him shivered.

A faint glow brushed his fingertips, like the start of applause.

He smiled, a little sadly. "Time for Act Two."

Chapter 10

The Great Escape

The morning began in whispers.

The dolls' house kitchen—usually a place of clinking thimble cups and polite chatter—felt taut, as though even the air knew something was about to break. The ticking of the toy clock filled the silence like a heartbeat.

Wendy leaned close across the doll-sized table. "We do it tonight," she said. Her voice was low, fierce. "When he leaves."

Ray nodded, sleeves rolled up to his elbows, lipstick still immaculate but eyes edged with fatigue. He tore a square of peeling wallpaper from the wall and spread it out flat. "A heist in miniature," he murmured, sketching a map with the burnt end of a matchstick. "Trapdoor here. Workshop floor there. Somewhere out there—answers."

Judy stood by the sink, silent, her hands tight around a tiny teacup. "You'll never make it far," she said finally. "He always comes back sooner than you think."

Ray gave her a quick, dazzling smile. "Then we'll move faster than he thinks. Someone has to try."

"What about Jack?" Wendy asked.

Judy glanced toward the sitting room, where the little boy slept curled beneath a tea towel, thumb in his mouth. "I'll stay with him," she said softly. "You two go. If you find a way out—bring help."

Ray reached across and squeezed her hand. "We'll bring more than that, love. We'll bring the curtain down."

When the evening came, the world outside the dollhouse dimmed into a dusky amber. The vast shadow of Valentino moved past the workshop window—then vanished. The click of the lock echoed like thunder.

Ray exhaled. "Showtime."

He and Wendy pried open the trapdoor beneath the dollhouse stage. A cold draft blew up from below. The passage was narrow, the wood rough against their fingers. One after another, they squeezed through, emerging into the cavernous expanse of the workshop.

It was like stepping into another world.

The air smelled of varnish and candle wax. Dust motes drifted in golden beams of light, each one huge as a feather. Tools the size of gallows hung from the walls. Half-finished marionettes dangled from racks, their glass eyes gleaming faintly in the dark.

Wendy shivered. "Feels like they're watching."

"They are," Ray murmured. "Waiting for something."

"Waiting for us."

They moved carefully, the floorboards like vast plains beneath their feet. Every sound—the creak of wood, the drip of water from a paint jar—felt magnified, alien. Ray's satin gown trailed behind him like a violet comet. He'd torn the hem for easier movement, but it still shimmered faintly as they went.

They found the radio first.

It sat on a workbench, the size of a building to them, whispering static. Ray climbed up using a spool of thread and a splintered ruler, his breath coming hard. "Let's see what's playing on the late show," he muttered, and kicked the switch.

The crackle turned to sound—human voices, too loud, too real. He fumbled to turn it down, and then, beside it, noticed the small television on standby. A faint red light blinked in the gloom.

"Help me with that plug, love," Ray said.

Wendy wedged the broom splinter beneath the switch. The screen burst into life, flooding them with pale blue light. They froze.

A newsreader's voice cut through the static: "…search continues for missing eight-year-old Jack Stevens, last seen near Torquay Pier…"

The picture changed—crowds, police tape, the tear-streaked face of a woman clutching a photograph. "Please," she sobbed, "please bring my son home."

Wendy's hand flew to her mouth. "That's his mum."

Ray felt his throat close. "He's not a character," he whispered. "He's a boy."

The television droned on—talk of volunteers, of hope fading. Then the image flickered, and the sound faded back into static.

For a long moment, neither of them spoke.

It was Wendy who saw the pinboard.

A scatter of papers half-hidden beneath sketches of puppet rigs and mechanical joints. She climbed the corner of the desk, brushed aside a hanging marionette arm, and froze.

"Ray…" she breathed.

He joined her—and the blood drained from his painted face.

There they were. Newspaper clippings yellowed and curling at the edges. Cabaret Couple Brian and Judy Vanish After Show, Missing Woman: Wendy Worthington, 34, last seen leaving Seaview Snacks Café. Another beneath it—Local Entertainer Ray Ramondo Vanishes After Cabaret Show.

"That's us," Wendy whispered. Her voice trembled. "and Brian and Judy thought they were forgotten, but they're not!"

Ray looked higher. Older cuttings—1963, 1970, 1977, 1982, 2006. Performers, actors, singers. Each one smiling in their photo. Each one missing.

"He's been doing this… for years." Wendy gasped.

Then he spotted it. At first, it looked like a forgotten corner — dust, cobwebs, scraps of broken puppets. But as Ray brushed away the grime, shapes began to emerge.

Tiny crosses. Dozens of them.

Some made of matchsticks, others from bent pins. Beneath each, a scrap of faded ribbon or a lock of hair, tied with care.

Wendy covered her mouth and stepped closer, her voice barely a whisper. "Oh God. It's a graveyard."

Ray knelt beside one, tracing the carved initials with trembling fingers: M.L. — 1963.

"They were like us," he murmured. "Actors. He shrank them, used them — and when they stopped performing…"

He couldn't say the rest.

For a long moment, they couldn't speak.

The only sound was the faint hum of the workshop lights and, somewhere distant, the slow tick of the clock.

A sound behind them.

The faintest rustle, then a low, delighted laugh.

Then, a shadow fell across them.

"Going somewhere, my shining stars?"

They turned. The light above blazed. Valentino stood over them, vast, elegant, terrible—his expression perfectly composed, his eyes bright with fury and delight.

Ray stumbled backward. Wendy pushed him behind her.

Valentino's gloved hand reached down; the air shuddered as invisible strings whipped downward like serpents. They coiled around Ray's arms, Wendy's torso, yanking them upward.

"Such betrayal," Valentino said softly. His voice carried no shout—just calm, glacial disappointment. "You wander, you pry, you question my art. Do you think yourselves heroes? You are only actors. And actors, my dears, must obey their director."

Ray fought the pull, the strings biting into his wrists. "You can shrink us, darling," he gasped, "but you'll never make us small."

Valentino's smile returned, cold and exquisite. "Oh, I don't need to make you small," he said. "You already are."

With a flick of his wrist, the strings snapped them downward.

They woke in glass.

A display case—its walls smeared with fingerprints and dust. Around them lay fragments of old marionettes, broken limbs, painted eyes staring lifelessly out. The "green room," Valentino called it once. An actors waiting room.

Through the glass, they saw him gliding away, whistling a low tune. "Consider this a rehearsal for obedience," he murmured, and disappeared into the dark.

Wendy slumped against the wall. "He's going to kill us."

Chapter 11

The Performed Morning

Morning came without comfort.

The first hint of light slid between the warped shutters of the tiny seaside theatre, casting crooked lines across the velvet curtains and the rows of seats. Inside the dolls' house, the world smelled faintly of damp wood and greasepaint, like a stage that had never truly rested.

Brian sat with his knees pulled up to his chest. Judy stood rigid by the miniature vanity, dabbing her face with a rag that seemed too small even for her tiny hands. Little Jack stared into nothing, his eyes wobbling, mouth trembling as if any moment might break him.

The silence between them was too thick, too heavy, too knowing.

No Ray.

No Wendy.

Judy swallowed hard and whispered, "They must have made it. Got beyond him. Gone for help." But she didn't sound convinced. She sounded like someone trying not to collapse.

Brian scratched his chin with shaking fingers. "Maybe they did. Maybe they're already at the police station. Or, or—maybe they woke up. Maybe this is all some sick dream." He didn't believe that either. The crack in his voice gave him away.

Jack sniffed once and rubbed his sleeve across his eyes. "They'll come back," he whispered. "They're stronger than him."

Judy touched his shoulder. "Let's hope so. Let's just—"

She didn't finish the sentence. She didn't need to.

Because then the roof of the dolls' house lifted off.

And there he was.

Valentino.

His pale face hovered above them like a cruel god evaluating his creations. Thick, bushy eyebrows drawn together, examining them. He smiled without warmth, eyes glittering with the sort of satisfaction a cat wears after cornering something tiny and alive.

"Good morning, my little ensemble," he purred, voice syrupy and venomous at once.

The three remaining actors froze. Valentino let the silence stretch, tasting it. Then he spoke, perfectly casual:

"If you are wondering about Ray and Wendy…" He paused, his gaze sweeping the miniature room. "They tried to escape at dawn. Silly, really. They should know by now that this world ends only when I say it does."

Jack sobbed once, raw and small.

Brian clenched his jaw.

Judy's eyes narrowed, like coals catching flame.

Valentino continued, "Do not trouble yourselves further. They have been retrieved, and they are… in rehearsal." The pause after that final word was horrifying.

He leaned closer, lowering his voice so it slithered between each of them.

"I would strongly advise no one else attempt such futile theatrics. I value loyalty. Disloyalty, however—" His smile sharpened, thin as a razor. "—gets rewritten."

Judy held Jack close, shielding his face with her trembling fingers.

"Now," Valentino said brightly, as though discussing something trivial like breakfast, "We have a matinee today. A cheerful one! The seafront patrons are waiting. You will perform your roles precisely as rehearsed."

He snapped his fingers.

Strings dangled, descending. Their strings.

The moment the threads touched them, something invisible but irresistible pulled at their limbs. Their bodies jerked upright against their will, like marionettes answering a silent command.

"It's Oliver Twist today," Valentino announced. "Dare I remind you, Judy, you are Nancy. Brian, you are Sykes. Jack—dear, sweet Jack—you are Oliver."

Jack whimpered, "I don't want to—"

Valentino gave the slightest twitch of a finger, and Jack's knees cracked down onto the wooden floor. He cried out in pain and Judy rushed to his side.

"You will," Valentino murmured. "And you will smile."

He lifted the roof back into place, sealing them inside.

They were marched onto the miniature stage.

The theatre interior was absurdly detailed. Red velvet curtains. Painted backdrops of the seaside. Audience pews carved from balsa wood, filled with silent faces—patrons from the town above, perched like children around a toy.

The house lights flickered.

Valentino's unseen hand tugged.

They began the performance.

Jack stepped forward, his little feet striking the boards as though dragged by a ghost. His voice trembled through the first verse of Food, Glorious Food, though his face carried a frozen grin he neither chose nor recognised.

Brian, as Sykes, took his place and sang the booming lines about hunger and longing, his voice quivering.

Judy followed, her tone soft and mournful as Nancy, her eyes wide with secrets. Between her lines, she dared tiny additions:

"Help…..We're…trapped…"

Her voice cracked. The audience leaned forward, smiling, charmed by what they thought was eccentricity. But no one in the audience heard anything except novelty.

Jack looked out into the bright human faces towering above them, and for a heartbeat hope flickered—someone might notice. Someone might see past the spectacle. Someone might understand.

Then Valentino's voice boomed—not aloud, but inside them.

Enough.

The strings yanked.

Jack's body jolted like a puppet tossed down a staircase. Judy's arm snapped upward, pinned at a grotesque angle. Brian's head jerked sideways with a sickening crack. And the audience applauded—thinking it was choreography.

"Encore!" someone cried.

Jack sobbed mid-song, voice warbling.

Judy's tears rolled silently but her mouth kept smiling, pulled like a cut stitched badly back together. Brian's eyes stared straight ahead, unblinking, as though forced to watch himself drown. Their strings gleamed like spider silk in the stage lights, so many little threads of power, control, imprisonment. The song trailed to an end.

The applause thundered. The curtains drew in, swathing them in crimson darkness. And all three tiny actors thought the same desperate thing:

What if Ray and Wendy never come back?

What if escape is impossible?

What if this stage is forever?

Chapter 12

Sparks and Shattering Glass

The world inside the glass case was quiet—too quiet. Dust floated like smoke in the pale strip of moonlight from the workshop window. Wendy sat with her back against the glass, knees drawn to her chest, staring at the shelves beyond. Ray stood beside her, peering through the cloudy surface as though he might somehow blink himself free.

Outside, the workshop was still. Every tool, every puppet head, every stray thread seemed to be waiting for a cue.

"You ever get the feeling," Ray murmured, "that the whole world's holding its breath?"

Wendy didn't answer. Her reflection trembled faintly in the glass, red light pulsing through the threads that rose from her shoulders. "I hate him so much."

Ray tried to smile, but it didn't stick.

In the glass, their reflections shimmered faintly—and then Wendy saw it. The thin strings rising from their backs glowed with a faint, pulsing red. Like veins. Like anger.
"What's happening to us?" she whispered.
Ray's hand found hers. His eyes burned. "We're waking up," he said quietly. "Curtain's not down yet."
Outside, from the forgotten television, Jack's mother's voice still echoed through the static. "Please… if anyone's seen him…"
The screen flickered, dimmed, and went dark. The latch on the workshop door clicked. Both froze.

Valentino entered.

He looked serene, composed—the calm of a man in perfect control. His movements were elegant, deliberate, every gesture rehearsed. He placed his gloves on the desk, adjusted his cufflinks, and lit the small lamp above the workbench. A circle of light bloomed in the dark.

"Another show," Ray whispered. "Front-row seats, lucky us."

Valentino prepared the space as if for ritual: a single chair angled toward the light, a neat stack of scripts on the table, a teapot steaming on a tray. Then came the knock.

"Enter," he called.

The door opened. A man stepped inside—broad-shouldered, ruddy-faced, the sort who filled a room by accident. His bomber jacket strained at the seams. "Evening," he said, flashing a grin. "Name's Glenn. Got your note about an audition?"

"Indeed," said Valentino, smiling thinly. "I've been searching for someone… formidable. A touch of strength. You might say—heroic."

Glenn chuckled. "You've found him, mate. Done bit parts in action films, a few adverts, gym promos. People say I'm a natural 'Rambo type.'"

"Perfect." Valentino gestured to the chair. "Sit. Let's see what you can do."

Ray pressed his face to the glass. "Oh, no," he whispered. "Not again."

Glenn sat, legs apart, hands on his knees. "Want me to do a monologue or something?"

"Something," Valentino said softly. "Yes."

He leaned back, watching with clinical fascination as Glenn launched into a booming speech about courage, fire, and battle. His voice filled the workshop, echoing off the shelves. Even Wendy flinched at the sound—it was too alive, too human.

When Glenn finished, Valentino clapped politely. "Excellent projection. Such… conviction."

"Thanks," Glenn said, grinning. "You want me to try another—"

"Tea?" Valentino interrupted smoothly. "You must be parched."

Glenn shrugged. "Don't mind if I do."

He took the delicate cup, dwarfing it in his hands. Sipped. "Not bad—bit floral."

Wendy's stomach turned. "Don't," she yelled, pressing her hand to the glass. "Don't drink it." Both she and Ray banged furiously on the glass, but their tiny taps proved pointless.

He couldn't hear. He took another sip, blinked—and swayed.

"Whoa," Glenn muttered. "What was in—"

His words slurred. The cup fell, smashing on the floor. He clutched the table, eyes wide and passed out.

Valentino rose, calm as ever, and opened a drawer. From it he drew a slender metallic rod—part wand, part instrument, faintly humming with blue light. He held it over Glenn like a conductor over an orchestra.

The light deepened.

Glenn's body began to shudder, shimmer—then contract. His limbs folded in on themselves, shrinking, his features warped like wax under flame. Within seconds, where the man had stood there was only a tiny figure in his crumpled jacket, twitching in confusion.

Wendy screamed.

Valentino smiled, crouched, and lifted the shrunken man delicately between thumb and forefinger. "Welcome to the company," he said, and carried him toward the dolls' house.

He placed Glenn gently inside on the sofa, where the others could see—and closed the roof. Then, humming softly to himself, Valentino gathered his gloves and coat, extinguished the lamp, and left.

The door clicked shut.

Silence fell like ash.

Wendy sank to her knees. "He's just going to keep doing it," she whispered. "Over and over. New faces, new toys."

Ray pressed his forehead to the glass. "You'd think I'd be used to rehearsing tragedy, but this…" His voice cracked. "This is cruelty on repeat."

She slammed her palm against the glass. "No more."

"Wendy—"

"No more!" Her voice rose, sharp enough to make the air tremble. "He thinks he can make us perform forever, but he's wrong. We're not his showpieces. We're people."

She hit the glass again. A spark flashed from her fingertips—just a flicker, but enough to startle them both.

Ray stumbled back. "Did you—?"

Wendy stared at her hands. Tiny arcs of light danced between her fingers, red and white like fireflies in a storm. Her breath came fast, shallow. "I can feel it," she said. "It's in me."

"Careful, love," Ray said, voice shaking. "You'll—"

"Help me."

He hesitated.

"Ray," she said, eyes blazing, "hands on mine. Now."

He obeyed. Their palms met against the glass—hers burning hot, his trembling cold. The faint hum filled the air again, rising in pitch. The cracks in the glass began to glow, veins of red threading outward.

Wendy closed her eyes, drew in a breath, and screamed—not in fear, but in fury.

The glass exploded.

Shards rained around them like crystal confetti, scattering across the wooden surface. The air buzzed with energy. For a moment, all sound vanished. Then Ray's laugh broke it—half hysteria, half wonder.

"Bloody hell," he gasped. "We actually did it."

They stumbled free, standing on the edge of the workbench, surrounded by shards that gleamed like starlight. The faint red glow still pulsed between their hands.

Wendy stared down at them, eyes wide with something that looked almost like awe. "We did that."

Ray nodded, breathless. "You did that."

She turned toward the dolls' house below. Through its tiny window, she could just see Glenn—motionless, trapped in the parlour. Beyond him, the flicker of Jack's lamp in the upstairs room.

"Now we know," she said softly. "It's not just his machine. It's us."

Ray followed her gaze. "So what's next?"

Wendy looked toward the workshop door, her face hardening. "Next," she said, "we find out how far this power goes."

Outside, in the silence, a faint echo stirred—Valentino's humming fading down the corridor, distant, unknowing.

The two of them stood among the wreckage, breathless, alive, and—for the first time—hopeful.

Chapter 13

Curtain Call

Morning came slowly to the workshop.

A faint light crept through the blinds, turning the air to dusty gold. On the highest shelf, among the glittering shards of their prison, Ray and Wendy worked quickly, side by side. Ray hummed under his breath—something soft, nervous, defiant—as he gathered the fragments of glass into a thimble-sized pile.

"If he walks in and sees this," he muttered, "we're deader than disco."

Wendy scanned the nearby shelves. "Not if he doesn't know what he's seeing."

She reached for another glass case—slightly smaller but the same shape—and placed it exactly where theirs had stood. From a lower shelf, she pulled two old marionettes, cracked and dusty, their faces roughly human.

"Those poor sods," Ray murmured. "They look how I feel."

"Good," Wendy said briskly. "Then they'll pass for us."

They stripped the puppets, swapped their own doll clothes onto them, and arranged them inside the case. Under the dim workshop light, the illusion was uncanny. From a distance, they might as well have been asleep.

Ray stepped back, admiring their handiwork. "Convincing. From tragic leads to set dressing in one night. How the mighty have fallen."

Wendy's lips twitched. "Not yet they haven't."

She turned to the drawer where Valentino kept his wand. The metallic hum still seemed to linger in the air. She grasped the handle and pulled—but it didn't budge.

"Move," she said through gritted teeth.

Ray winced. "Darling, brute force has never—"

The drawer snapped open with a crack, splinters flying. Wendy stood there, breathless, a faint shimmer tracing her fingertips. Inside, nestled among wires and velvet cloth, was the wand.

Ray whistled. "You're getting good at this."

"Getting started," she said. Together, they climbed into the drawer, heaving the wand between them. It was heavy, almost as long as Wendy's arm, faintly humming with stored power.

They carried it back to the shelf, where the imitation glass case gleamed faintly in the light. The wand's plug dangled over the edge of the bench. Wendy dragged a piece of thread, looped it around the cord, and lowered it carefully to the socket below.

A spark jumped. The hum returned, low and steady.

They crouched behind a spool of thread, waiting.

Down in the dollhouse, Judy sat beside Jack, who stirred fitfully in his tiny bed. She'd been awake all night, listening for footsteps that never came.

"Ray and Wendy, they're not coming back," she said quietly. "He caught them."

Brian paced the floor, running a hand through his hair. "They were reckless. Always thinking they could change the script."

"You think we should just accept this?" Judy snapped.

Brian rounded on her. "I've been thinking, look at it this way Judy. We've got a roof, a stage, applause, and top billing. There are worse ways to be forgotten."

Glenn, sitting awkwardly in the corner, scratched his head. "I dunno," he said slowly. "Doesn't feel right, does it? He ain't normal, that bloke."

"No," Judy said. "He's not."

Jack appeared in the doorway, rubbing his eyes. "Where's Ray?" he asked sleepily.

Judy gathered him close. "He's… busy, sweetheart."

Brian muttered, "Busy getting us all killed."

Outside, the first sunlight hit the workshop window.

The lock turned.

Ray and Wendy froze as the door opened. Valentino swept in, coat flaring, humming an aria under his breath. He set down his cane and gloves, face aglow with artistic delight.

"Ah," he sighed, "a new day, a new performance."

He moved to the shelf.

Ray's pulse raced. "Now or never."

Valentino reached for the glass case, peering in at the motionless puppets inside. "How obedient," he murmured. "At last, a little stillness."

Wendy rose behind the spool, the wand gripped tight in both hands. She met Ray's eyes. He nodded.

He flipped the switch.

The hum deepened, the air rippling like heat haze. The wand vibrated in her hands. She dropped it—let it fall past him.

It hit the floor with a flash of light.

Valentino staggered. His elegant posture faltered. He looked down at his hands—already shrinking, the skin paling to porcelain, his movements jerky, marionette-like.

"No," he hissed. "No—this is my stage—"

His voice fractured into a shrill, distorted echo, the words warping as reality folded around him. He shrank—inch by inch, heartbeat by heartbeat—limbs folding inward, coat collapsing in ragged pleats. With every breath he grew smaller, his authority draining from him like colour washed from old silk.

The room loomed monstrously around him now; the floorboards stretched like a wooden continent. The ceiling soared like a cathedral vault. Valentino looked up—far, far up—at Ray and Wendy towering above him as if they were the giants he'd always feared they could become.

He had shrunk past their size. Past the dolls' size. Past anything remotely powerful.

At last, he stood amid drifting dust motes—tiny, perfect, still conscious. A living marionette stripped of strings.

His eyes widened with disbelief, then terror. "No… no, this isn't possible—this isn't how the story goes!"

Wendy and Ray climbed down from the bench, hearts pounding but steady now, each step shaking the tiny ground beneath him.

Ray crouched, studying Valentino with something like morbid curiosity. Then he plucked him delicately between finger and thumb, holding him as though he were nothing more than a lost toy and effortlessly bound his hands and feet.

"How the mighty tumble, darling," Ray whispered.

"Untie me!" Valentino screamed, his voice brittle as cracked glass. "You fools—you don't understand what you've—"

"Oh, we do," Wendy said softly, stepping closer, her eyes dark with the quiet thrill of victory. "We understand perfectly."

She leaned in, her breath stirring his shrivelled coat. "We didn't just break the story, Valentino." Her smile was slow and razor-thin.

"We took back the show."

They returned to the dollhouse like conquering heroes, carrying the wand between them and the wriggling figure of Valentino bound in a spool of silver thread.

Judy gasped. "You did it."

Ray grinned, setting the miniature villain on the table. "Encore, anyone?"

Glenn stepped forward, squinting at the wand. "That's the gadget, is it? Looks electrical. Let's see what makes it tick."

He examined the base, turning a dial marked with strange, glowing symbols. "This thing's adjustable. Maybe we can reverse it."

"Careful," Judy warned. "You don't know what you're doing."

"Sure I do," Glenn said cheerfully. "I was an electronics engineer once. Can't be that different, right?"

He pointed the wand at a nearby egg in an egg cup. "Science time."

Wendy held her breath. The hum started low, then built until the air quivered. The egg shimmered—and in a sudden burst of light, it expanded to full size, smashing through the table.

Ray whooped. "It works!"

They looked at each other—then at the wand.

Brian looked disappointed. "I dunno folks, it's a lot to give up. I'm a star, my names in lights ….."

"You're a little star Brian and your names in little lights!" Judy snapped.

"I can't believe you're even considering staying.…now, step into the light".

Brian did as he was told.

Moments later, one by one, the pulse of light grew stronger. The room seemed to fold around them, the walls stretching outward, colours blurring. When it cleared, they were standing in the workshop once more—life-sized, trembling, human. Wendy stared at her hands. Flesh and bone. Real. "We're back."

Jack cried out in wonder as he grew beside them, his pyjamas billowing around him. Judy and Glenn followed—stumbling, blinking, alive.

Ray threw back his head and laughed, loud and glorious. "Oh, sweetheart, I've never been so thrilled to be middle-aged and mortal."

"Now what?" Glenn asked.

Wendy looked down at the tiny figure of Valentino, no bigger than a toy soldier. He stood on the table, still shouting orders to no one.

Ray tilted his head. "You thinking what I'm thinking?"

Moments later, Valentino was inside a birdcage, strung from the ceiling by a length of ribbon. His tiny fists beat against the bars.

"You'll regret this!" he squeaked. "I am art! I am eternal!"

"Of course you are, darling," Ray said sweetly. "You'll be the talk of the town."

They stepped back, the others watching in stunned silence as the little figure swayed, the cage turning slowly in the morning light. His voice faded to a manic giggle—half defiance, half applause.

Ray smiled faintly. "You wanted a captive audience," he murmured. "Now you've got one."

The cage turned once more, glinting gold.

Epilogue

– Torquay, Tuesday

MISSING BOY RETURNS HOME!

Jack Stevens, the eight-year-old who vanished from Torquay Pier, has been safely reunited with his parents. The boy, who was reported missing two weeks ago, appeared "in perfect health" and told reporters he had been "on a big adventure with new friends." When asked about his plans for the future, Jack said he hopes to "be an actor one day — maybe even a magician."

The Stage & Screen Gazette

FIVE ACTORS REAPPEAR AFTER MONTHS AWAY

Believed missing, the five performers have returned home — and announced plans to form a new theatrical troupe. The group, calling themselves The Dolls' House Players, said their absence had been "an extraordinary creative sabbatical." Their debut production, Strings Attached, is expected to tour the South-west next spring.

New Scientist

'MINIATURISATION BREAKTHROUGH' PATENTED BY BRITISH TEAM

A group of five actors and a young boy are believed to have developed a machine capable of reducing the size of living organisms and inanimate objects. Filed under the name The Valentino Reduction System, the technology has reportedly drawn attention from several government departments for "potential large-scale applications." Sources suggest the inventors "will never have to work again."

No. 10 Downing Street – Official Statement

PRIME MINISTER APPROVES PRISON MINIATURISATION SCHEME

In an effort to reduce overcrowding across the HM Prison Service, the government has authorised the implementation of the Valentino Reduction System for both current and future inmates. "This innovation will literally shrink the size of our prisons," a spokesperson said. "Thousands of offenders will now serve their sentences in facilities no larger than a tennis court."

TV News – Special Report

FIRST SHRUNKEN PRISONER TRANSFERRED TO 'NEW WORMWOOD SHRUBBS'

Former theatre producer Patrick 'Valentino' Larkin has become the first inmate to undergo the miniaturisation process. Sources confirm he has "adjusted well" to his new environment and has submitted a formal request to establish an inmate theatre troupe to "uplift morale through performance." The Home Office is said to be "considering the proposal."

Footnote:
If you're wondering about Wendy and her special powers, she's asked to keep them strictly under wraps. Still, audiences swear the stage literally lights up whenever she's on it — though she insists it's just good lighting, a bit of make-up and good old East End Pie and Mash!

The End

The Man Who Knew Everything

Chapter 1

Malcolm Green was the sort of man who couldn't let a fact go uncorrected.

He didn't argue to win — he argued to exist.

It wasn't arrogance, he told himself.

Just civic duty. Someone had to keep the world accurate.

If someone said the moon was made of rock, he'd correct them: "Technically, it's regolith."

If someone used "irony" wrong, he'd sigh, "That's actually coincidence."

If someone told a story, he'd already know how it ended — because he'd read about a similar case somewhere, sometime, tucked away in an article he kept bookmarked in his mind. Facts, to Malcolm, were companions: steady, obedient, always there when people were not.

He worked for East of Englands's Morfolk County Services — Policy Administration — though he preferred to say "strategic oversight."

It sounded cleaner, sharper, more suited to the man he believed himself to be. His desk was a fortress of mugs, printouts, paperclips arranged by size, and post-it notes covered in facts, none of them useful.

His favourite read: Did you know you can't hum while holding your nose? He told people this at least twice a week, then demonstrated.

No one ever laughed.

Still, Malcolm persisted. In his mind, the world depended on the steady drip of corrections he offered it. Without him, it would slide into chaos.

Even boiling water became a lecture.

"Actually, you shouldn't pour boiling water straight onto the teabag," he told Rebecca from Accounts one morning.

"It burns the leaves. You want just-off-the-boil — ninety-three degrees."

Rebecca smiled, left her tea unfinished, and started using the upstairs kettle instead. The one in the far corridor. Behind two fire doors.

Malcolm noticed. He told himself she simply preferred the pressure there.

At the Thursday pub quiz, Malcolm was both an asset and a liability. He knew everything — except when he didn't, and then he'd argue until closing time.

"Capital of Mongolia?" asked the quizmaster.

"Ulaanbaatar," said Malcolm. "Though if you knew your phonetics, it's Oo-lan-baa-tar. There's a glottal stop—"

"Two points," said the quizmaster.

"Two? Surely one, it's only one word," Malcolm insisted.

The room groaned. His team, The Smartinis, never won.
They always came second — victims of Malcolm's corrections, his clarifications, his determination that even leisure must be accurate.

"Malc," said Gary, his teammate, after one exasperating round, "we're here for the beer, not your bloody thesis."

Malcolm smiled thinly.
"That's exactly the attitude that holds this country back."

Gary ordered another pint.

Even his neighbours avoided him.

When the couple next door installed a smart meter, Malcolm appeared at the fence, arms folded, ready to educate.

"It's all alternating current, you see. The electrons don't move down the wire — they just vibrate."

"Right," said the husband, gripping a barbecue tong like a weapon.

"But the National Grid's synchronisation—"

The patio door shut before he could finish.

Malcolm stood there a moment longer, nodding to himself.
People these days didn't appreciate knowledge.

He lived alone now, though not unhappily. His ex-girlfriend Vicky, had once told him, "You're impossible to talk to."

He'd replied, "That's because you're emotional, not logical."

She'd left the following spring.

His son stopped calling soon after. Malcolm sent him links instead — job articles, nutrition studies, quotes from successful men. Replies dwindled to single words, then stopped entirely.

Still, Malcolm told himself he was misunderstood, not disliked.

"They can't handle accuracy," he muttered one night over a microwave curry. "That's the problem with this country. Everyone prefers to be wrong together than right alone."

The fork tapped against the plastic tray as he ate. The flat hummed faintly with the sound of the fridge.

He found comfort in the order of his small routines: bedtime at eleven, lights off at eleven-oh-eight, the faint glow of his screensaver looping through photographs of galaxies and obscure historical figures.

Certainty. That was what mattered.
A world built of facts, lined up properly, waiting to be deployed.

At work one Tuesday, his manager mentioned that "three out of four residents" supported the recycling scheme.

"Actually," said Malcolm, without looking up, "it's sixty-two percent. It was in the Echo last week."

"Really?" the manager smiled. "That was the 2022 survey. It's seventy-six now."

A small laugh went round the table. Someone whispered, "Malcolm got one wrong."

He smiled politely, but the comment lodged somewhere deep.
A small crack.

That evening he checked.

Seventy-six percent.

It shouldn't have mattered — but it did.
A percentage was meant to be fixed, verifiable, unchanging.
Instead, he found himself scrolling between sources:

Sixty-eight.
Seventy-two.
Sixty-one (adjusted for seasonal variation).
None agreeing.

He read the methodology.
He read footnotes.
He read the statistical caveats at the bottom of every page.

For the first time in years, certainty slipped.

The numbers didn't add up.
The graphs contradicted themselves.
Facts — his foundation — seemed suddenly unstable.

He rubbed at his temples, annoyed at the unfamiliar thrum of doubt.

By midnight, his flat glowed with the light of three screens.

When did Henry VIII die?
1537.
1538.
1539.

He clicked again.
The answers changed.

Once more.

Different again.

He stared, frowning, waiting for one version to assert itself.
Facts were facts — they didn't just alter because someone phrased the question differently.

"Ridiculous," he said aloud. "People will believe anything."

He reached for the radio to drown out the noise of his thoughts.
A phone-in on BBC Norfolk was mid-discussion about conspiracy theories.

"No one knows everything," said the host. "That's part of life's mystery."

Malcolm smirked.

"Speak for yourself."

Chapter 2

The plane touched down in Quito just after dusk. The air was thin and crisp — high altitude, low humidity — and Malcolm explained this loudly to the woman in the seat beside him as they taxied to the gate.

"Most people don't realise oxygen concentration drops by almost a third up here," he said, tapping his temple. "That's why you feel light-headed. Simple science."

She smiled tightly, unclipped her belt, and moved to an empty row without a word.

The arrivals hall was a riot of colour and noise: families waving signs, taxi drivers shouting over one another, the sharp scent of coffee drifting from a stall to the left. Malcolm found it all very invigorating — almost cosmopolitan compared to Norwich Airport, where the most exciting sight was a delayed flight to Amsterdam.

He paused to read every poster on the wall.

"Altitude sickness… hydration… sunscreen at high elevations," he murmured. "All very sensible."

He corrected a nearby tourist — loudly — on how to pronounce Cotopaxi, then made sure two others knew that llamas and alpacas were "often confused by the uninformed."

By the time he reached baggage claim, three people had moved to stand elsewhere.

The taxi ride proved no more restful.

The driver began politely: "Welcome to Quito, señor. Beautiful night, yes?"

"Technically," Malcolm said, adjusting his seatbelt, "the perception of beauty is subjective, though the night sky here is clearer due to reduced air pollution."

The driver nodded uncertainly.

"And by the way," Malcolm added, "it's Quito — short 'i'. Not 'Kee-toh', as the guidebooks incorrectly imply."

The driver's smile grew fixed.
Malcolm spent the rest of the drive offering unsolicited commentary on altitude, colonial architecture, and the comparative efficiency of Latin American traffic systems.

By the time he reached his hostel — El Cóndor Feliz, a lime-green building wedged between two internet cafés — Malcolm had already corrected the taxi driver's pronunciation, given advice about gearboxes, and attempted to tip using British coins.

The receptionist, a young woman with a nose ring and limitless patience, asked what brought him to Ecuador.

"Research," he said. "Cultural. Educational. I like to immerse myself."

"Ah," she replied kindly. "Very brave."

Malcolm did not notice the look she exchanged with her colleague.

His room was small but bright, decorated with woven blankets and a carved wooden condor perched above the door. Malcolm examined every object.

"The Andean people have a rich textile tradition," he narrated to himself. "Fascinating craftsmanship. Bit dusty, but still."

He spent twenty minutes reading the emergency exit instructions, red pen in hand, annotating several grammar errors.

By the next morning, he had settled comfortably into local life — or so he believed.

He woke early, stepped outside, and launched himself into the streets with the enthusiasm of a man in search of admiration. Quito obliged him with a cacophony of markets, music, clattering buses, and the smell of grilled corn.

He bought fruit from a stall, explaining to the vendor the difference between plantains and bananas ("a matter of starch content, you see").
He interrupted a tour guide to point out that the equator was "not exactly where the tourist line indicated."

He warned a pair of backpackers not to drink unfiltered water — then drank a glass of it himself to "build immunity."

Within twenty-four hours, the locals had begun calling him Señor Profesor.

He rather liked it.

He spent his days wandering the narrow streets, notebook in hand, pointing out architectural details and sharing small facts in slow, careful English.

To his surprise, people listened.

A museum guide thanked him for "the correction about the English expedition."
A café owner clapped him on the back after hearing about coffee beans technically being seeds.
A group of teenagers asked for a selfie after he explained the volcanic ring of fire.

Everywhere he went, he found respect.
Deference, even.

It was intoxicating.

For the first time in years, Malcolm didn't feel like a nuisance.

He felt important.

He felt heard.

By the end of the week, people sought him out in the plaza to ask questions.
Tourists stopped him for advice.
A small local paper ran a photo captioned El Inglés Sabio – The Wise Englishman.

He cut out the article and folded it neatly into his passport.

In the evenings, he held court in bars filled with music and cigarette smoke. Locals leaned in, laughing at his confident chatter about volcanoes, global economics, and the correct way to brew English tea.

When someone asked what he did for a living, he smiled, lowering his voice.

"Let's just say… government work."

It sounded better than Policy Administration.

"Ah!" one man whispered. "Secret service, yes?"

Malcolm chuckled, enjoying the mystery.

"I couldn't possibly comment."

He meant it playfully.

They did not take it that way.

Over the next two days, he noticed things he chalked up to coincidence:

A man in a brown jacket appearing at every café he visited.
A black car idling too long outside the market.
A woman who took a photo of him, then quickly walked away.

"Tourists get mugged, not kidnapped," Malcolm muttered. "Statistically speaking."

But he tightened his backpack straps all the same.

At the Saturday craft market — overflowing with bright fabrics, carved masks, and pots of fruit glistening like jewels — Malcolm noticed the man again.

Same jacket.
Same distance.

He told himself not to be paranoid.

He turned down a side street — narrow, quiet, the air warm with the smell of ripened fruit.

A van screeched to a halt beside him.

Hands — rough, fast — grabbed his arms and dragged him in.

He tried to shout, "I'm a British citizen!" but the words came out muffled against the sack pulled over his head.

The last thing he saw was a crushed mango rolling into the gutter.

Chapter 3

When he woke, it was dark.
The air smelled of damp concrete and petrol.
His wrists were bound with cable ties. Somewhere close, water dripped steadily — plink, pause, plink — like a clock mocking him.

A voice in Spanish asked a question he didn't understand.

Another voice translated, haltingly: "You work for the English government. Tell us what you know."

Malcolm's heart hammered. He wanted to say he worked in recycling statistics. But the thought of admitting ignorance — of being wrong — was unbearable.

So he nodded. "Yes," he said, steady as he could. "I know things."

He made it up as he went.
Details about submarine cables, coded weather forecasts, hidden outposts in the Falklands.
He even quoted from a James Bond film, thinking it lent authority.

They took notes.

They asked for diagrams.

Malcolm, terrified and trying to sound professional, drew rectangles and arrows on a scrap of cardboard and labelled them things like OPERATION SEABASS and CHANNEL 12: RESTRICTED ACCESS.

When the kidnappers finished transcribing every mark, they photographed the diagrams and sent them up the chain — to El Jefe, the head of the cartel.

El Jefe, who fancied himself a pragmatic businessman, didn't waste time. He forwarded the images through an encrypted contact to his man in London with a message:
"For your government. Five million pounds or he dies."

Within hours, the drawings sat in an MI6 inbox in Vauxhall Cross.
A junior analyst opened the files, blinked, and frowned.

"What the hell is this?"

The room filled with murmurs.
Boxes labelled 'Seabass', arrows to nowhere, and notes like 'High tide = clearance window'.

An internal memo followed:
"No known operation matches. Possibly a decoy. Possibly... gibberish."

The analysts scrolled, baffled. Someone suggested it looked like an educational flowchart. Another swore they recognised the handwriting from a 'How To Write Clearly' government workshop.

After twenty minutes of confusion, the British reply came back through channels:

"We have no idea who this man is. And whatever he's selling — it's nonsense."

When the message reached the cartel, silence filled the room.
Then came the shouting.
Then came the fists.

Malcolm tried to explain the concept of "plausible deniability."
That's when they hit him.

By the fourth day, he was half-delirious.
When they shouted questions, he corrected their grammar.

"Not 'what you know,' it's 'what do you know.' Verb before subject."

They didn't appreciate the lesson.

Somewhere between the fifth and sixth interrogation, he stopped trying to make sense of it. He started muttering to himself, the way he used to at work.

"People don't want the truth," he said. "They only want to be right."

Back home, the story made headlines.

LOCAL COUNCIL WORKER KIDNAPPED IN ECUADOR – BRITISH AUTHORITIES BAFFLED

Old colleagues were interviewed.
"Malcolm was very clever," said one. "Just not... situationally."

Vicky, his ex-girlfriend, appeared on breakfast television.

"He never knew when to stop," she said. "Even when he didn't know what he was talking about."

A photo of Malcolm — smiling awkwardly at his council desk, laminated recycling poster behind him — appeared on every screen.

In the dark of the cellar, Malcolm heard rats scratching behind the wall. He smiled weakly. "Rodents of the genus Rattus norvegicus," he whispered. Facts were comfort. Facts were home.

He recited capitals, chemical symbols, dates — each one a small act of control against the dark. But as the hours bled together, he began to suspect something.

Some of the facts didn't sound quite right anymore.
He'd whisper, "The capital of Mongolia is Ulaanbaatar," and hear a faint echo — a second voice, patient, correcting his pronunciation.

He blinked into the darkness, then a thought struck him. Malcolm Green wondered if knowledge might not be power after all. It might just be bait.

The cell smelled of damp concrete, rust, and old sweat — something sweetly rotting too, the ghost of a crushed mango left in a corner. Water dripped somewhere behind the wall, counting seconds in a language only the building knew. A single strip-light buzzed above, the sound thin as a fly's wing. Malcolm lay on the floor with grit in his knees, the concrete cold through his trousers. Night and day blurred into one grey smear, and his certainties, for the first time, began to feel thin.

Then the voices came.

Not a chorus, no theatrical whispering — more like radio static that coalesced into words. The sound had texture: a voice like a tinny broadcaster, half-tuned between stations.

"So you thought you knew everything…"

He pressed his forehead into the stone as if that would muffle it.

The memory of Vicky's mouth moving through that old phrase was a scalpel now, cutting close.

"Couldn't bear to be wrong… a bore to others… admit it, Malcolm. You talk too much. I can't get a word in edgeways… You're impossible."

Her final words just as she left him. But he felt dazed, confused, and his muddled brain wondered if he ever knew a Vicky?

He clamped his hands over his ears and chanted, silently, a litany of specs and dates like talismans. He tried to make a fact hold — the boiling point of water at sea level — and it returned thin, almost meaningless.

"Stop it," he whispered. "I've had a breakdown, that's all."

The voices made a sound like laughter, and the wall of the cell seemed to shiver.

"What would you do with such knowledge?"

He writhed until his ribs ached. In the dark he saw flashes of other small humiliations: his boss smiling while saying "two weeks" in the canteen; colleagues slipping away from his corrections. Each image dug at him.

When dawn seeped under the door, pale as skimmed milk, his clothes were damp with sweat. He sat up and something inside him had shifted. Where before there had been nervous stutters and hinge-loose certainties, there was now a horrible, intoxicating clarity.

Information arrived — not learned but downloaded: dates, scores, street names, chemical symbols — neat, exact, relentless. The brain that had stumbled over phonetics now ticked through data with an almost painful efficiency. Letters made little grids behind his eyelids. Sounds sharpened into trivia. Thoughts clicked like typewriter keys.

He thought, privately, of the guard's boy and the red bicycle his neighbours had mentioned in passing; the image came vivid and specific, and Malcolm felt a guilty flutter — as if the thought itself had been an intrusion. He bit the inside of his cheek to stop himself speaking. The knowledge was there, hot and bright, and he dared not let it out.

Days passed in a blur. The facts multiplied like mice: the hum of a light bulb and the likely voltage behind it; the genus of mould clinging to a damp corner; the precise angle of the sun at high noon over Quito.

Then the foreign memories arrived. They were not echoes of his life but photographs slid under his skin with surgical precision. He saw a murder he'd never witnessed — the curve of a knife, the pattern of blood on a living-room carpet — and held the details like grocery lists. He named things no sane man ought to name: quiet military projects, outposts, dates of deaths. The images lodged there without permission.

One of them stayed with him: a small coastal town at dusk, gulls wheeling, a man pushed from a pier into black water. The detail of the pier's splintered railing burned in his mind. It was precise and wrong, not his memory but present as if someone else had pressed it into his skull. He tried to tell himself it was nonsense. The image sat like a stone.

The knowing grew less like a trick and more like a tide. He could predict the colour of the next car to pull up outside the gate. He could tell, before it happened, which song the radio would play.

But purpose rotted at the core. These "memories" of murders, secret bases, dates of deaths — they arrived unbidden and left him hollow. He was a receiver, not an author.
He wondered if the world's knowledge was leaking — and he was the crack.

Practical thinking returned like a muscle memory. If this torrent continued and he displayed it — if he let the guards, the cartels, governments pick at him — he would become currency. Useful meant bargaining chips; bargaining chips meant deeper holes and harsher questions.

He assessed risk like a man writing policy again. He practised errors, feigned confusion, let silence spread like fog.
He'd always despised small talk — now it was camouflage.

Outside, far from concrete and rats, the world kept its quiet business. Inside, Malcolm's mind hummed on, sharp and terrible as a clock wound too tight.

And that was when the thought came.

If knowledge had been bait, then pretending not to bite was the only defence he had. Malcolm Green, the man who had once believed the world needed correcting, now rehearsed the opposite: the gracious, grateful fool. He closed his eyes and recited silently a list of capitals and saints and boiling points — a lullaby of certainty to buy him a little more time.

If he was going to survive, he couldn't show them what he knew. He had to play stupid. Pretend the miracle hadn't happened. Keep the voice quiet.

Malcolm Green — the man who thought he knew everything — would have to relearn the oldest trick in the book.

He'd have to act ignorant.

For once in his life, that might just save him.

Chapter 4

The room was smaller than his cell — a box of concrete and shadows, with a single drain in the floor and a chain bolted to the chair leg. The walls sweated moisture; the ceiling was stained with the dripping patterns of years. A single bulb flickered in the centre, its wire swaying slightly as if moved by breath rather than air. The place smelt of bleach and iron — an antiseptic attempt at civility laid over something older, darker.

Malcolm's wrists were bound in front of him, the plastic cuffs biting just enough to remind him of his pulse. Every time he shifted, they rasped against his skin like serrated teeth. His ankles were free, but the chain fixed to the chair leg made even the smallest movement awkward. He could feel grit under his shoes and a faint tackiness on the floor where blood had dried long before his arrival.

He counted the seconds between each drip from a leaking pipe.
Six. Seven. Eight.
He clung to the rhythm as if it were oxygen.

Be ordinary. Be stupid. Stay alive.

The door opened with a slow, deliberate scrape. A rectangle of harsh light cut across the floor, stretching toward him like the tongue of some waiting beast.

A man entered — tall, suited, and the kind of clean that suggested other people scrubbed on his behalf. His dark hair was slicked back without a strand out of place. His shoes gleamed unnaturally in the dimness. His left index finger bore a fresh cut that hadn't quite stopped bleeding, the bead of red bright against his immaculate cuffs.

"Señor Green," the man said, his English careful but clear. "You know who I am."

Malcolm blinked twice. Blink too slow, he might look calculating; too fast, unhinged. "A dentist?"

The man's mouth gave the smallest twitch — amusement or fury, Malcolm couldn't tell.

"We know you work for your government."

Malcolm gave a small, nervous laugh. "Local government," he said. "Refuse collection."

One of the guards snorted. The interrogator did not.

"You are not garbage man," the man said flatly. "We have friends who say you know defence secrets."

Malcolm shrugged, feigning confusion. "Well, we did defend recycling targets. Vigorously."

The guards laughed — a short, startled bark of relief. It was small, but it bought him precious air.

They questioned him for hours. The kind of hours that stretch the mind until it thins like old elastic. Sometimes he was struck — a sharp crack of a hand or the blunt thud of a fist — and sometimes he wasn't. The unpredictability was another tool.

The rhythm became almost conversational — a grotesque seminar delivered through clenched teeth.

"What is OPERATION SEA BASS?" the interrogator demanded.

Malcolm furrowed his brow, letting his mouth fall open slightly as though recalling something from a misplaced file. "That was a pilot scheme. Fisheries logistics. Very hush-hush."

"And PROJECT FIBRE?"

A small hesitation — not enough to seem rehearsed. "Thermal insulation research. Failed miserably."

He watched the man's pen scrape across paper. Every falsehood Malcolm fed them was wrapped in the language he knew best: meaningless bureaucratic jargon. He learned quickly how to lace falsehoods with official-sounding nothingness — references to "regional data clusters," "hydrological oversight teams," "budgetary compliance departments." Departments that existed everywhere and nowhere.

The interrogator's eyes gleamed with the thrill of supposed discovery.

"Very good," he murmured. "Now we begin to understand."

Malcolm, throat raw, nodded meekly. Once, he'd mocked colleagues who believed everything projected on a PowerPoint slide. Now he used the same tone — smooth, boring, authoritative — to stay alive.

Meanwhile, he catalogued everything in the room: the rusted bolts in the door, the slight drag in the interrogator's left foot, the guard with the nervous blink. Information settled into his mind like dust — unbidden, unwanted, unstoppable.

The transcripts moved up the chain within hours.

A translator typed them neatly in Spanish, double-spaced, adding occasional question marks in the margins. The file went to a man in a white linen suit who read them twice, frowning deeper each time.

He forwarded them to a "friend in Europe," who passed them quietly to an old contact at MI6.

In London, a grey analyst spread the papers across a desk under fluorescent light. He wore a shirt that had been ironed more by desk heat than actual effort.

"Green, Malcolm," he muttered. "Council administration, Norfolk."

A younger colleague leaned over his shoulder. "Either he's a genius playing games, or he's mad."

The analyst shrugged, scratching his jaw. "Both can be true."

He tapped at his keyboard, drafting the official reply:

Subject not known to us. Information without value.

The message travelled back the way it came — encrypted, translated, decrypted — slipping across borders like a rumour.

Three days later, when the interrogator next entered the room, his composure had cracked like thin ice.

He strode forward, flung the printed page onto the concrete in front of Malcolm, and hissed through clenched teeth:

"You make joke! They say you are nothing!"

Malcolm blinked at the page, feigning bewilderment. "Didn't they like it?"

The man hit him — an open-handed slap that stung more for the insult than the force.

"You are stupid," the interrogator spat. "Stupid, like a dog!"

The guards laughed again, louder this time — emboldened because someone else had set the tone.

Malcolm coughed, tasted blood, and managed a smile that he quickly turned into a pained grimace. Inside, a strange thrill stirred.

The performance was working.
For once in his life, being underestimated was a victory.

Later, dragged back to his cell, he sat against the wall and let the ache wash through him. His lip throbbed, but the pain grounded him — an anchor against the torrent inside his skull.

The facts still came, sharp and metallic, but he pushed them down. Survival now depended on silence, not speech.

He'd done it.
For now, at least, they thought him harmless.

Above, the light hummed its one long note — steady, officious, like a ceiling fixture in a council hallway. Below, water trickled toward the drain, curving around small imperfections in the concrete. Malcolm watched it snake along the floor, mapping routes the way he once mapped arguments in meetings.

A memory rose — himself, years earlier, leaning too far over the conference table, telling colleagues: "Ignorance is the seed of every disaster."

He laughed softly now, the sound dry as sand.

"Then let disaster bloom," he whispered.

The bulb flickered once — as if in agreement.

He closed his eyes and began crafting another lie — one neat enough, boring enough, and dangerously plausible enough to keep him breathing through another day.

What he didn't know was that somewhere in London, in a quiet office above the Thames, the same analyst who had dismissed him was now reading Malcolm Green's answers again — slowly this time. There were patterns buried in the nonsense, shapes in the bureaucratic fog. Hidden coordinates.

The analyst frowned, picked up the phone, and said to no one in particular:

"Find out who taught this man to lie so well."

Chapter 5

The room smelled of dried blood and fear.

Not fresh blood — no, that had an iron bite, sharp and bright. This was older, seeped deep into concrete and wood, the kind that clung to the back of the throat and refused to leave. Malcolm sat slumped in the chair, wrists raw where the cable ties had chewed the skin. Every small movement sent a sting up his arms. The metal legs of the chair were uneven, so it wobbled slightly whenever he shifted his weight — a maddening, pointless wobble that made the whole room feel unstable.

Above him, the single light buzzed like an irritated wasp. Its flicker was erratic: two long pulses, one short, a faint tremor, then darkness for half a second. Malcolm might have found the pattern interesting, even comforting, if it didn't feel like the bulb was deliberately choosing the most irritating moments to gutter.

Somewhere nearby, a tap dripped — slow at first, then faster, then slow again, never falling into rhythm. An irregular, syncopated beat that began sounding like a distracted drummer or a heartbeat fading in and out of death.

He'd stopped counting the hours long ago. Days, maybe. The men came and went in loops — shouting, silent, impatient, bored. Their moods shifted like sand in wind. Sometimes they entered laughing; other times one walked in already rolling up his sleeves.

He remembered one backhand so sharp and sudden that stars exploded across his vision — actual stars, shimmering constellations dancing behind his eyelids. A strange, inappropriate pride flickered through him when he realised, he still knew the names of everyone.

Orion. Cassiopeia. Ursa Minor.

The knowledge grounded him. Even now.

That was when the voice came again — smooth, almost helpful, slipping into his thoughts like a hand guiding him toward an answer.

"This might help."

And suddenly he understood.

The Spanish pouring into his head wasn't noise anymore. It was organised. It had structure. Meaning. He heard phrases as though they were being translated inside his skull, slotting into place:

El Jefe's furious… three days… the car… the cocaine under the bonnet…

The knowledge aligned itself like cogs in a clock. The men in this outpost had stolen cocaine from their boss. El Jefe had found out. He was planning to kill them all in two days' time.

And they didn't even know it.

Malcolm almost laughed. A bubble of incredulous amusement rose in his chest. For once, knowing too much might actually save him.

The guards returned. Same two as before. One spat on the floor, the glob landing near Malcolm's shoe with a wet slap.

"You stupid donkey!" he snarled, the insult thick and clumsy.

Malcolm lifted his head slowly. Bloodshot eyes. Split lip. Measured calm.

Then, in perfect Spanish, he said:

"El Jefe sabe lo que hicieron."
El Jefe knows what you did.

Silence snapped through the room like a wire pulled taut.

The older guard's face turned chalk white. The younger's mouth flapped open like a startled fish.

"How does he know?" one whispered.

"I told him," Malcolm said smoothly, voice steady now. "He sent me to check on you."

The lie felt almost elegant — and terrifyingly plausible.

Malcolm let it hang there, heavy and unanswered.

The silence thickened, coagulating in the space between them. He could feel his own pulse hammering at the base of his throat, a dull, animal insistence, but he did not rush to smother it with words. He had learned—somehow, over years of small violences and smaller, quieter victories—that silence unsettled men far more deeply than shouting ever could. Silence invited imagination. And imagination, once stirred, did the work for you.

The older guard swallowed. His Adam's apple bobbed violently, like something trapped beneath the skin, trying to claw its way out.

Malcolm smiled then.

It was faint, almost apologetic, as a thought slipped neatly into place. There was no warmth in it. Not warmth. Never warmth. It was something adjacent to compassion but hollowed out—pity, perhaps, or the echo of it.

"El Jefe doesn't like surprises," he said softly. "Especially not messy ones."

The words settled badly.

A bead of sweat loosened itself from the younger man's temple and slid down the side of his face. He wiped it away with the back of his hand, smearing grime and panic across his sleeve. The room seemed to contract. The air soured. It smelled of metal and damp wool now—of uniforms worn too long, of fear soaked in and never quite washed out. Old fear. Familiar fear.

"What exactly does he know?" The older guard asked.

Malcolm stood.

He did not hurry. He rose as though time itself had obligingly slowed for him. When he took a step forward, the floorboard creaked beneath his weight—sharp, intrusive, far too loud in the quiet. Both men flinched as if struck.

"He knows you went off book," Malcolm said. "He knows you moved without clearance. He knows someone saw you."

"That's impossible," the younger guard said too quickly. "There was no one—"

Malcolm's eyes flicked to him.

Not anger. Not accusation.

Something colder. Precise. Surgical.

"That's not what I was told," Malcolm said. "You were seen. And reported."

The younger guard froze. His mouth opened, closed, useless as a broken hinge.

The older guard turned on him at once. "What did you tell him?" He hissed, venom threaded with terror.

Malcolm raised a hand, palm outward.

The gesture was almost gentle. Almost kind.

"You don't need to do this here," he said. "Not with me."

He moved past them then, slow and unhurried, as though the room belonged to him already. He examined it with idle interest. A cracked mirror spider-webbed with age. A cheap table, its surface tattooed with old knife marks—counted absently, catalogued. A chair overturned in the corner, one leg shorter than the others. He took it all in. Filed it away.

"El Jefe is deciding what to do," Malcolm continued. "That's why I'm here. To see whether you're assets… or liabilities."

The word dropped into the room like a gunshot.

The older guard sagged against the wall, suddenly ancient, his bravado draining out of him in one long exhale. "We followed protocol," he said weakly. "Mostly."

Malcolm turned.

"Mostly," he said, "is not a word that keeps you alive."

The younger guard's hands were shaking now. He pressed them together, knuckles whitening, as if prayer might still be accepted at this late hour.

"If he knows," he said, his voice splintering, "then why aren't we already—"

"Dead?" Malcolm supplied.

Both men stared at him.

"Exactly," Malcolm said.

He tilted his head, studying them—not their faces, but the fractures in them. The stress points.

"Because El Jefe likes context," he went on. "And because some men are more useful alive."

He paused. Just long enough.

"For example," he said lightly, "he knows you've been skimming off the transport runs. Small amounts. Careful amounts. Enough to feel clever. He knows about the cash buried behind the boiler in your cousin's garage."

The younger guard made a strangled sound.

"And you," Malcolm added, turning to the older man, "he knows about your son. The gambling debt. The way you've been paying it down with favors you were never authorised to give."

The room broke.

"Stop," the older guard whispered. "That's—no one told you that."

Malcolm's smile returned. Thin. Controlled.

"You'd be amazed what gets reported," he said. "Eventually."

Something in their expressions shifted then. Suspicion sharpened into something uglier. Predatory.

They were no longer afraid of El Jefe.

They were afraid of him.

And fear, when it realised its source was standing in the room, had a habit of turning violent.

By the next morning, they were calling him Señor Verde. One even brought him a plate of food — eggs fried too long, rice clumped together, and a slice of banana. It looked almost edible. In his state, it was divine.

They hovered near the door, nervous, curious, whispering questions.

"Does El Jefe forgive?"
"When will he call?"
"Does he… does he watch us now?"

Malcolm, bureaucratic to the marrow, replied in the tone of a mid-level manager updating a spreadsheet.

"Soon," he said. "He's watching. Don't make me write another report."

Their expressions shifted — fear, awe, pleading — and he could almost taste the power in the air. Bitter, shaky, absurd power, but power nonetheless.

On the second evening, the keys appeared on the metal table outside his cell. No ceremony. No speech. Just the younger guard placing them down as though delivering communion.

"Take it yourself," he murmured, voice thin.

Malcolm stared. Blinked twice, slow.
After all that… was it really that easy?

He stood, legs trembling from disuse, limped to the table, and picked up the keys. They were warm from someone's pocket. Heavy. Important.

He could hear the voice of some forgotten council trainer in his head:

Never waste a good procedural loophole.

Outside, the jungle greeted him like a damp, restless beast. Humidity clung to his skin, thick as syrup. Mosquitoes whined near his ears. Leaves rustled without wind, as though things moved behind them.

The battered Toyota sat waiting, bonnet weighed down by secrets.

He opened the door — slow, steady — and sat behind the wheel. The seat was cracked, stuffing poking through like exposed bone.

He turned the key.

The engine coughed — a dry, reluctant bark — then shuddered as though reconsidering the effort. For a breathless second it seemed it might die there with him. Then it caught, settling into a low, obedient purr that vibrated up through the steering column and into his bones.

He drove.

The dirt road stretched ahead, a narrow, treacherous vein carved through the trees. Mud spat up against the sides of the car, thick and black, peppering the doors like thrown stones. Branches reached in from the dark, scraping along the roof and windows like fingernails testing for purchase. Somewhere beneath it all, something rattled loose in the dashboard, keeping time with his heartbeat.

Too loud.
Everything felt too loud.

His hands were slick on the wheel. He did not wipe them.

Not a mile down the road, the night fractured.

Headlights flared through the trees — bright, hard, unyielding. White spears cutting between trunks and undergrowth, advancing with purpose.

Black jeeps.

Several of them.

Moving fast.

Malcolm's breath snagged painfully in his chest. He swerved off the road without thinking, tyres sliding in the mud, then killed the lights. The car vanished into darkness. He stayed perfectly still, crouched low over the wheel as the engine ticked softly while it cooled, each metallic click sounding like a countdown.

The jeeps thundered past.

Their engines hummed with a disciplined menace, like insects bred for war, fat on blood and certainty. Mud sprayed in their wake. Inside, men sat rigid and composed, uniforms pressed, collars clean. Too neat for this place. Too coordinated. Their faces were blank, stripped of curiosity, stripped of mercy.

Professionals.

A few heartbeats passed.

Then came the sound.

The stuttering crack of automatic fire split the night — short, controlled bursts. No panic in it. No waste. Just enough to end whatever needed ending.

The sound echoed once, then was swallowed by the trees.

Silence rushed in behind it, thick and absolute.

Moments later, the jeeps returned the way they'd come, tyres chewing the road to slurry, windows blacked out, secrets intact. They did not slow. They did not look back.

Malcolm remained frozen until the last tremor faded from the ground.

Only then did he exhale.

The breath left him in a long, careful stream, ghosting the air like steam from a cooling body.

"Well," he murmured to the empty road, voice barely more than a thought, "that's one way to end a meeting."

When the night finally loosened its grip, and the road lay empty once more, he turned the car around.

And headed back.

The house was quiet now. Too quiet. Smoke drifted from an open doorway in thin, sickly tendrils. Somewhere inside, a radio still played a cheerful song — strangely high-pitched, dancing above the metallic scent of fresh death.

The men lay where they'd fallen — bodies twisted, eyes staring into nothing. No loyalty remained in them, only surprise.

Malcolm stepped over one, tugged off its jacket, and changed clothes. The shirt was still warm. It smelled of sweat and cheap cologne.

In the kitchen, he found a drawer full of passports — his among them.

Typical.

He pocketed the others, slid his into the dead man's shirt, and scattered a few of the books they'd kept in his cell — cheap paperbacks with curling covers — across the corpse.

Convincing enough.

He stood in the doorway for a moment, surveying his own manufactured death.

"Not bad for a man without an NVQ in espionage," he muttered, and stepped into the humid dark.

He drove until dawn. The jungle slowly thinned into scrub and open road. Birds cried overhead. A warm breeze brushed his face.

The voice in his head were quieter now, replaced only by the steady rattle of old mechanics and the churn of tyres over cracked earth.

For the first time, he was free, or at least, not currently tied to anything.

He found that strangely comforting.

London.

The briefing room was pale and overlit, scrubbed to a colourless neutrality that made every face look faintly unwell. Fluorescent panels hummed overhead with a thin, constant whine, the sound of restrained power — electricity caged and civilised. It could not have been further from the jungle if it had tried.

Three MI6 analysts stood spaced apart like chess pieces, coffee cups cooling untouched in their hands. Beside them sat a woman from Morfolk County Services, jacket still on, expression set somewhere between irritation and fatigue. She had the look of someone who had been dragged into matters she did not believe should exist at all.

A satellite feed filled the wall.

"That's the location," one of the analysts said, tapping the screen with a pen. "Visual confirmation of the compound."

The image was stark. A grey square scorched into green nothingness. Roof collapsed inward. Walls blackened, skeletal. The jungle pressed close, already reclaiming the edges, vines threading through ruin like veins seeking a pulse.

"Are we sure Green's alive?" Another analyst asked, squinting at the magnified frame.

A pause.

"Doubtful," the first replied. "There's a body matching his description. Height. Build. Clothes. Passport. The lot."

The word lot landed with bureaucratic finality.

The council woman folded her arms. She didn't look at the screen for long. "Typical," she said. "Always leaves a mess behind."

No one challenged her.

The MI6 lead straightened, smoothing invisible creases from his suit. "We will send the retrieval team regardless," he said. "If it is him, we bring the body home".

Silence followed. Not fear. Not surprise. Just acceptance.

They all stared at the frozen image — the burned-out house, the scorched earth around it, the faint line of tyre tracks slicing north through the jungle before dissolving into foliage.

No one asked where the track led.

No one suggested following it.

Elsewhere — far beyond the reach of satellites, committees, and retrieval teams — Malcolm Green was already several hundred miles away. The road beneath him was cracked and empty, the sky vast and indifferent. He hummed softly under his breath, tuneless, almost content, as the city he would never return to receded into irrelevance.

A map of locations, trails, and villages zipped through his head — routes unfolding, distances calculating, dangers annotating themselves in real time. Information poured in, relentless and exact. His hands responded without thought, coordinating with the wheel as though guided by something other than instinct, driving him on, driving him forward, driving him toward freedom.

Chapter 6

The sky above Tenerife was the kind of blue that made people forget wars, debts and bureaucracy. Down in Los Gigantes, the sea was a sheet of polished glass, sun-punched and lazy, a perfect mirror for the steep black cliffs that rose like sleeping giants from the shoreline. Holidaymakers moved like slow, colourful beetles along the marina walkways, their chatter drifting in faint bursts of laughter and clinking glasses. It was, in every sense, a place designed for forgetting.

On a wide terrace that caught every drop of the afternoon light, a man reclined on a white sunbed beside an aquamarine pool. The water shimmered with small ripples, disturbed only by the warm breeze that carried the scent of suncream, salt, and lemons from somewhere in the villa's kitchen.

A bottle of Tanqueray sweated quietly on the table beside him.

Malcolm Green — though not, technically, Malcolm Green at this exact moment — stirred the ice in his glass with lazy satisfaction, the cubes chiming pleasantly. His skin, once pallid from East Anglian drizzle, now bore a modest golden tint. His hair, once flattened by office ceilings and cheap council-building radiators, lifted lightly in the warm breeze. His toes, visible beyond the sunbed, flexed in a peace he'd never found in Norfolk.

He sighed — a long, blissful sigh that felt almost indecent.

From the kitchen came the hum of conversation: two voices, low and rhythmic, discussing seasoning for fish. The sound of a lemon being halved followed, the bright, citrus tang joining chlorine in a strange but agreeable perfume. It was, Malcolm thought, the very height of civilisation. Sunshine. Solitude. Gin. The absence of policy meetings.

He closed his eyes and let the warmth sink into his bones.

There was a knock at the villa door.

He didn't move. "Get that, will you, Miguel?" he called, still reclined, the picture of a man who had absolutely no intention of answering his own front door ever again.

Footsteps crossed the tiled floor, and for a moment all was quiet — the hush before the reveal.

Then a familiar voice boomed from the hallway.

"Señor Samuel!"

Malcolm — or rather, Señor Samuel — sat up with a grin already forming, adjusting his sunglasses as a tall, well-dressed man stepped onto the terrace. The sunlight caught the gold in his cufflinks, throwing back a sharp gleam.

"El Jefe!" Malcolm said warmly. "Always my pleasure to see you."

They embraced — not theatrically, but with the understated confidence of two old colleagues who shared profits, secrets, and the occasional near-death experience. Malcolm felt the slight press of the man's cologne, expensive and heavy, like sandalwood warmed by the sun.

"And you too," said El Jefe, stepping back to admire the view. "The villa has wonderful views. You have chosen well."

Malcolm lifted his glass in a small salute. "Always good to be home."

El Jefe's smile thinned as he took in the man before him — healthy, whole, and no longer shackled in a concrete cell far beneath South America. His eyes softened with something like pride.

"You look well, considering. Apologies for the implant, by the way," he said lightly, as though apologising for a delayed dinner reservation. "We also had a few technical hitches which we thought might throw you?"

Malcolm huffed a dry laugh. "There were moments," he admitted. "For a moment I completely forgot about my supposedly ex — Vicky." He gave an exaggerated shudder. "Poor woman. She didn't exist 'til you put her in my head. Then she wouldn't stop talking."

El Jefe chuckled. "Artificial Intelligence is still in its early days, and has a mind of its own sometimes. Next time, you'll see much improvement."

Malcolm grinned and rubbed the back of his neck where the faint scar still tingled beneath the skin. The memory of the surgery flickered — sterile lights, the cold press of metal, the hum of power as something alien slid into his skull, bringing a storm of knowledge with it. "Apart from the punches," he said dryly, "the implant was the worst bit."

"The next one," El Jefe said, pouring himself a drink, "will be a microchip. Implanted in your neck. Gentle like a kitten."

Malcolm barked a short laugh — the dry, knowing laugh of a man who had spent years correcting people and had now discovered the incomparable joy of choosing not to. "Let's not use Norfolk Council again, eh?" he said. "Difficult people. Full of self-importance."

El Jefe nodded gravely. "No. We have our eyes on central government now. Westminster. You shall have the perfect identity."

The wind shifted, carrying the soft wash of the ocean against the cliffs and the distant cry of a gull. Malcolm set his empty glass down, watching the sunlight glitter on the pool's shifting surface. Two reflections looked back at him — broken, doubled, wavering in the light. It felt fitting.

The two men raised their glasses.

"To a job well done," El Jefe said.

"To believable incompetence," Malcolm replied, tapping his glass to El Jefe's. "Without which this entire enterprise would be impossible."

They drank.

Inside the villa, the living room was cool, tiled, and sparsely furnished. A map of South America hung on one wall — nothing marked, but already filled with memories in the minds of both men. On the opposite side, a map of Europe. Someone had circled Westminster in faint pencil.

El Jefe wandered toward the kitchen while Malcolm followed at a slower, contented pace. Miguel had prepared a plate of fresh papaya and lime, which now sat on the counter beside a stack of documents bound with a plain elastic band.

Malcolm plucked a piece of papaya and chewed thoughtfully. "So," he said, "tell me. How did the British take it?"

El Jefe raised an eyebrow. "As expected. They believed everything."

"Everything?" Malcolm repeated, pleased.

"They dismissed your diagrams as nonsense — which, of course, they were." He poured himself more gin. "But they were nonsense with just enough shape, just enough pattern, that someone began to look closer. To question. To wonder what kind of man could compose such convincing rubbish."

Malcolm brightened. "A man with an implant glitch?"

"A man who will soon walk the halls of Whitehall," El Jefe corrected gently.

Malcolm chuckled and bowed his head in mock modesty. "Well, far be it from me to deny my country the pleasure of my expertise."

"Your next country," El Jefe said pointedly. "You must remember — Malcolm Green will soon become someone else. Someone useful."

"Someone who knows everything?" Malcolm teased.

El Jefe's lips curved. "Someone who knows exactly what we want him to know."

The sun dipped lower as the afternoon wore on, drifting lazily toward the horizon. Shadows lengthened across the terrace. Miguel brought out plates of grilled dorada and vegetables slick with olive oil, setting them beside a bowl of fresh bread.

Malcolm sat back, enjoying his new life with a serenity that would have horrified his former colleagues.

"You know," he mused between mouthfuls, "I was worried the persona wouldn't hold. Ex-wife, estranged son, the whole 'lonely man with a superiority complex' thing."

"You played it well," El Jefe said.

"I am a lonely man with a superiority complex," Malcolm reminded him helpfully.

El Jefe laughed and clapped him on the shoulder. "The world will believe what it wants to believe. That is why you are perfect."

Malcolm smiled. There was no malice in the expression — merely a quiet, satisfied confidence.

"And the chip?" he asked, tapping his temple. "Still faulty?"

"For now." El Jefe shrugged. "But it worked well enough. You understood languages you never learned. You sensed danger before it came. You filled your lies with details we never taught you. Imperfect technology is still technology."

Malcolm nodded slowly. "It did whisper strange things sometimes. As though someone were... tuning it. Adjusting?"

El Jefe's expression didn't change. "A minor issue. Easily fixed."

Malcolm accepted this with a shrug. Terrifying whispers, phantom memories, sudden bursts of knowledge — all part of the job.

"You did well," El Jefe said, raising his glass again. "The British believe you are dead or worse: incompetent. Perfect conditions."

Malcolm gave a small, self-satisfied smile. "Ignorance," he said, "is the seed of every disaster."

El Jefe laughed. "Do not plant too many, Señor Samuel. We need them alive long enough to listen to you."

Malcolm reclined once more, letting the twilight settle over the terrace. The cliffs glowed deep orange. The ocean darkened to ink.

For a long moment, neither man spoke.

Then Malcolm sighed. "You know," he said lightly, "I am rather proud of myself."

"Good," El Jefe replied. "Because we begin again soon. And next time, my friend..."

He leaned in, his voice dropping.
"…you truly shall know everything."

Malcolm smiled into the fading light — calm, clever, utterly at home.

The man who had once corrected teabag temperatures was now preparing to correct a government.

And this time, the world would listen.

The End

Thank you for reading……

We hope you enjoyed The Healthiest Corpse in the Morgue and other stories,

If so, please do leave a review on all your preferred platforms to help spread the word!

Arabella Parke

About the Author

Arabella Parke has always been drawn to the quiet thresholds—those fragile borders where the implausible brushes against the everyday and dares to feel real. She believes the world is threaded with hidden whispers, subtle shifts, and the soft, unmistakable hints left by those who have already stepped beyond the veil. To her, the departed are never truly gone; they linger in glances, in instincts, in the small decisions we convince ourselves we made alone.

Guided by these unseen currents, Arabella writes stories where the ordinary loosens its seams to reveal the strange beneath. Her work explores the shadows we sense but seldom name, and the eerie grace of the past as it reaches its hand into the present.

Special Thanks.

Thank you to those around me who make me laugh — who fill my days, and these pages, with wit and delight. I am fortunate to be surrounded by lively humour, sharp comedy, and the kind of laughter that brings sunshine to my days. You know who you are, and the credit is entirely yours.

Much appreciation to Terry and James, for putting up with the constant tapping of keys, late dinners, and the occasional burnt one — your patience has not gone unnoticed.

Special thanks to my dear dad, Peter Jackson, who gave me the title for this book. Gifted with an original mind and an effortless wit, he could fill any room with laughter. Heaven has gained a little more joy, and a lot more mischief.

Printed in Dunstable, United Kingdom